"Felicity," Mother's voice interrupted. "I'm so glad to see you've returned from dancing. Your father and I would like to introduce you to someone."

Felicity looked across the table at Zach, who only raised his eyebrows as if to say, "I told you so."

"He comes from a fine, upstanding family," Mother continued, completely oblivious. "And his father has several long-standing investments in the mining and refinery businesses."

So this is what Mother had meant when she said she and Father had been working hard on something. Why did they feel the need to be so secretive? Why not come right out and tell her what they were planning? Felicity wanted nothing to do with Mother and Father's matchmaking schemes. But she owed it to them to at least pretend to go along.

She took a deep breath and turned to face the unknown man.

"Felicity Chambers, I'd like to introduce you to—"

"Brandt!"

AMBER STOCKTON is a freelance Web designer and author whose articles and short stories have appeared in local, national, and international publications. Other credits include nine contributions to *101 Ways to Romance Your Marriage* and two contributions to Grit for the Oyster as well as an article for Christian Fiction online magazine. She is a member of American Christian Fiction Writers and a board member for her local ACFW chapter. She is married to fellow author, Stuart Stockton, and lives in beautiful Colorado Springs. Their first baby was born in March. Visit her Web site to learn more or contact her at www.amberstockton.com.

Books by Amber Stockton, writing as Amber Miller

HEARTSONG PRESENTS
HP784—Promises, Promises
HP803—Quills and Promises
HP823—Deceptive Promises

Copper and Candles

Amber Stockton

Heartsong Presents

My top appreciation goes to my husband and my family on both sides for their unfailing support. Thanks also to my editors, JoAnne Simmons, Rachel Overton, and April Stier Frazier. I'd be lost without all of you! Supreme gratitude to my heavenly Father for the gift and joy of writing. It's a blessing to reach so many readers and touch lives through this creative outlet.

A note from the Author:
I love to hear from my readers! You may correspond with me by writing:

Amber Stockton
Author Relations
PO Box 721
Uhrichsville, OH 44683

ISBN 978-1-60260-340-0

COPPER AND CANDLES

All scripture quotations are taken from the King James Version of the Bible.

All of the characters and events in this book are fictitious. Any resemblance to actual persons, living or dead, or to actual events is purely coincidental.

Our mission is to publish and distribute inspirational products offering exceptional value and biblical encouragement to the masses.

PRINTED IN THE U.S.A.

one

Detroit, Michigan, April 1875
Near the business district

Felicity Chambers brushed sweat-soaked tendrils off Lucy Gibson's forehead. "Make sure you get some rest today, Mrs. Gibson. I don't want to return after work and find that you have overtaxed yourself."

The woman offered a weak smile, not even bothering to open her eyes. "I will."

The strain of a recent fever had taken its toll on the woman's frail body. Felicity's charity work involved delivering meals to the Gibson home. When complications developed from Lucy's pregnancy at just four months, the woman was forced to quit work at the candle factory. How could Felicity turn a blind eye to the need?

To her left another girl a couple of years younger than her nineteen years managed to corral the youngest boy of five children and get him settled in his high chair for breakfast.

"Marianne," Felicity said over her shoulder, "Timothy has been told that if you should need anything at all today, you are to send him to the factory to find me." She smiled at the thought of Lucy's oldest, the scrappy, quick-witted lad who had secured a place in her heart at her first visit to this home.

"Yes, ma'am." The young girl bobbed her head then turned her attention back to the toddler in her care.

Marianne lived two doors down and came to care for the home and children. With Lucy bedridden at the doctor's orders, Marianne was needed now more than ever. The other four children, ranging in age from three to eleven, scampered around the small house. Soft giggles and exclamations followed them. At least they showed respect for their mother's condition. Their shoes had holes and their clothes were a bit ragged, but they had a warm house and food in their bellies. With their mother unable to work, all of that would be taken away. Felicity couldn't let that happen.

On impulse she had sought employment at the factory and promised to give Lucy her wages. Felicity had grown tired of the constraints of her life of luxury. Working at the factory afforded her the chance at adventure without Mother dictating what charity work to do and overseeing her every move. For the first time in her life, she had a feeling of independence. She had chosen this work, and it felt good. It had seemed like the perfect solution. But now she wasn't so sure.

Grabbing her lunch pail and shawl for warmth against the cool spring morning, Felicity stepped outside and pulled the creaky, splintering door closed behind her. She smoothed a hand down the coarse fabric of her borrowed clothes. So different from the fine silks and linens she normally wore.

Am I ready for this?

Taking a deep breath and offering a silent prayer, Felicity stepped through the whitewashed gate with the chipped paint and hooked the latch. No sense prolonging the inevitable. And despite her reservations, she actually looked forward to this change of pace. Her charity work allowed her to see how less fortunate and struggling individuals lived.

But this! Working in a factory as a commoner, side by side with other girls nearing twenty or younger? It was almost more than she ever could have imagined. She'd wanted a change of pace from the never-ending parade of teas, invitations to come calling, and other social functions. And now she had it.

As she walked east toward the business district, Felicity took note of her surroundings. Small homes, some on the brink of collapse, lined both sides of the street. They were so close together it was hard to imagine the residents having any privacy. She thought about her own town house on the northwest side of the city. Healthy, green lawns and impressive gardening at the front and rear accented the brick three-story house with black shutters. A wrought-iron railing flanked both sides of the seven marble steps leading to the front door. Quite a difference from the overgrown cement and sometimes dirt paths that led to the fronts of these homes.

Felicity left the residential area and entered the business district. Only this part of the district wasn't anything like where she'd been with her father on more than one occasion. She quickened her pace to a brisk walk. It wasn't the first time she'd been in areas similar to this, but she still needed to be on her guard.

Garbage littered the ground at almost every turn. The disgusting odor forced Felicity to breathe through her mouth instead of her nose. She would have held a handkerchief over her face, but she'd left it at the Gibsons' with her personal belongings.

Her eyes watered at the acrid stench of decay. If she wasn't overcome by the smell, she might make it far enough to escape this part of the city. Felicity averted a mangy cat that looked like he hadn't eaten in weeks. Barking dogs and the screech of another cat from a nearby alley joined with the shouts of some of the street vendors hawking their wares.

"Customerrrr, come he-re!" called the singsong voice of a traveling vendor who walked beside his cart, laden with items of every shape and size imaginable.

Never in her life had Felicity seen so many different types of people clustered together in one place, nor so many faces reflecting despair and sad acceptance. Did her efforts even make a difference? She had so much, and they had so little, yet they seemed to work hard despite their circumstances. The sooner she moved past this area, the better. Felicity didn't know how much longer she could endure the cacophonous sounds and heartbreaking sights.

She turned right at the next intersection, relieved she had almost reached the area near the factories, when raised and heated voices just ahead of her drew her attention. Stopping in her tracks, she took note of five men facing off in the middle of the street. Three of them stood face-to-face against the other two, and by the looks on their faces, the words they spoke were anything but friendly.

An inner voice told her to keep moving, but the prospect of a possible fight drew her like a child reaching out to touch a hot stove. She'd heard of brawls from her older brother, but she'd never witnessed one firsthand. And the thrill of danger was too tempting to ignore.

"I said I'd teach you a lesson with my fists if I caught you on my turf again."

This came from the shortest of the five men, but what he lacked in height, he made up for in bravado.

"And I told you we wasn't on your turf. Your man here"—the one on the defense pointed at a brawny man beside the first one who spoke—"he told you we was. But he should get his eyes checked."

The big man referenced swore loudly and took a step forward, but the shorter one held him back. Felicity gasped at the profanity.

"It's my word against yours," the first man countered. "And I say you *was* on my turf."

"I say we settle this right here and now."

More expletives came from both sides. Felicity had only

heard *of* these words. She'd never been present to hear them spoken. No wonder Mother kept her sheltered.

Felicity held her breath. She looked around to see only a handful of kids and a few spectators who had gathered. Everyone else went about their business as usual. Why didn't someone stop this? Did they not care? But instead of stepping away, she edged closer, drawn into the small crowd.

No sooner had she settled in place than the shortest man threw the first punch with a sickening thud. Felicity gasped and covered her mouth. It was three on two, unfair odds in her estimation, but the two seemed to handle themselves fairly well. The crack of fist on flesh and bone made her cringe and close her eyes. She peered through one eye and then the other, almost not wanting to know how the fight progressed.

As one man tackled another and rammed them both into the ground, Felicity jumped back. The violence had begun in a small area, and it now expanded as the men swung at and dodged each other. Well-placed blows knocked them down and widened the circle of their dispute.

All right. She had seen enough. Why any man would lower himself and engage in this type of atrocious, animalistic behavior was beyond her. Felicity stepped back and turned away from the ghastly sight. She had almost made it to a vacant lot when the thump of one body hitting another caused her to look over her shoulder—just in time to see a man flying in her direction.

❧

Brandt Lawson ran down the garbage-littered street, the thud of his scuffed leather shoes on dirt keeping time with the frantic beat of his heart. He'd be late if he didn't hurry. He turned the corner only to have the wind knocked out of him as his forward motion suddenly changed direction. His lunch pail flew from his grasp. Sailing through the air for what felt like an eternity, Brandt hit the ground—hard.

It took him a few moments to catch his breath and clear his head. Vague awareness filtered through his mind as the shock wore off. Movement on top of him made him open his eyes. He propped himself on his elbows. Pain shot through his shoulder. As he tried to inch backward, he saw the mass of dark tresses splayed out on his chest, some pinned in a haphazard fashion on top of the woman's head while others tumbled free from their confinement.

"Mmmm."

The mumble came from somewhere within the tangle of hair, and the female form on top of him shifted. His senses took over, and he placed his hands around her as he attempted to move into a sitting position. Unable to do so with the weight of the other person, Brandt instead slid out from under her and kneeled beside her.

The young woman's head rolled to the left and right, but she didn't open her eyes. At least she looked all right. Then again, Brandt had absorbed the majority of the impact. He glanced around to see what had caused her fall and saw the unruly bunch of men fighting not ten yards from where he and the young woman now rested.

Great. Just what he didn't need. He was already running late for his meeting before work, and now he had to be interrupted by a street fight. All attention from the crowd was focused on the men. Except for one young boy. The lad stood halfway between them and the group of spectators, his eyes wide and his mouth open.

Brandt turned his attention again to the young woman and smoothed back the hair from her face.

"Miss?" He patted her cheek a few times. "Miss, are you hurt?"

She stirred beneath his touch. Her eyelids fluttered then opened. She blinked several times, as if trying to gauge her surroundings. As soon as she focused on him, she sat up with a start and placed one hand on her chest.

"Dear me! I must apologize. Are you the person who broke my fall?"

Brandt opened his mouth to reply, but the lyrical, polished sound of her voice left him speechless. It stood in direct opposition to the fashion of clothing she wore. The young woman didn't seem to notice, though, as she continued with her ramble.

"It happened so suddenly." She swept one arm outward in an arc around her body. "One moment I was minding my own business and walking to work. The next I stopped to observe a shocking display of immature behavior." Her gaze stretched toward the ongoing fight. "Before I knew it, one of the men came flying toward me. I tried to escape, but to no avail." She looked back at him, her hazel eyes soft and apologetic. "If it hadn't been for your opportune presence, I might have suffered a more serious injury."

Opportune? Brandt wasn't sure he'd call it that. In fact, it couldn't have happened at a more *in*opportune time. He would have told her that if it hadn't been for the way her head tilted to one side as she regarded him. A dimple in her cheek appeared just to the right of her mouth, and she scrunched her eyebrows together in a most appealing manner. With a glance downward, Brandt realized she still sat in a heap on the ground. He silently scolded himself as he stood and extended both hands to her.

"Forgive me for neglecting my manners. Can I help you up?"

One corner of her mouth tugged upward, and amusement danced in her eyes. She offered her hand to him and accepted his assistance. When they were both on their feet facing each other, Brandt almost took a step back. Her head fell a few inches shy of his own. He stood just over six feet. He'd never encountered a young woman only four inches shorter than him.

But as much as he would have liked to stay and get to know more about her, duty called.

"I'm sorry to rush off, but I was already late when we ran into each other. And now unless I run I have no hope of getting to my meeting on time."

"There is no need for an apology. It's my fault for choosing you as my cushion instead of the street." She glanced again to the group of men who were the real cause of the delay and grimaced. "If it hadn't been for my curiosity, neither of us would be in this predicament."

And what a predicament it was. Under other circumstances, Brandt might have been more upset. But he didn't mind such a charming young woman being the additional reason for his tardiness.

He regarded her with a curious eye. "Well, as long as you're all right."

She dusted off her skirts, tugged down the edge of her blouse, and reached up a hand to touch her hair. A grimace crossed her delicate features, followed by a resigned shrug as she no doubt realized the tangled mess was a lost cause.

"I'm fine. I assure you. Now off with you before the number of minutes you're late is beyond excuse."

Brandt bent to retrieve his cap from the street and slapped it on his head. When he turned, he kicked the pail at his feet. How could he forget his lunch? He grasped the handle and looked up. The young lad who had been watching them raised his arm, another bucket dangling from the boy's fingers. Thrusting the one he held toward the young woman, Brandt nodded his thanks to the boy and took the other pail.

As he started to dash off, he turned his head and called over his shoulder. "I hope your day ends up being better than it started."

The echo of her giggle reached his ears and made Brandt smile for the first time that morning. When he left the house after breakfast, his father had reminded him for what felt like the thousandth time that he was expected to do his best at the refinery. He had dismissed the admonition with an absentminded wave, but he'd obey his father's demands. Like he always did.

As he ran toward the grouping of factories along the river, Brandt reflected on his life. Focusing on that kept his mind off the reprimand he was bound to receive when he arrived late. He would soon assume his father's place and take charge of the family investments. But first he had to learn what it was like to work at all levels, not just in management. Despite the inconvenience, the edict was a sound one. How else could he truly understand those who worked for him when he had never been where they were?

Brandt slowed as he reached the outer gate. Once past the entrance, he jogged toward the refinery, eager to begin his day and hoping the bumpy start this morning wasn't a sign of things to come.

His father's foresight in setting up this meeting and seeing to every aspect necessary continued to impress him. He hoped he'd be able to fill those shoes well when the time came. Approaching the manager's entrance to the refinery, he pushed open the door and stepped inside. Brandt was supposed to meet with one of the supervisors this morning before work to go over some of the details of his new job. He had a difficult balance to strike ahead of him. While performing as an average refinery worker, he also had to continue increasing his knowledge about the management end. He needed to make a good impression on both counts. And now he was fifteen minutes late.

If only he hadn't stopped by that music shop on his way

to work. He might have been able to get the young woman's name or at least find out where she was headed. But then again, if he had taken the original path he'd planned, he wouldn't have been at that corner at that precise moment. And they never would have met.

The chords of the guitar mixed with the tonal sounds of the accordion had called to him. He couldn't ignore it. His love of music had made him take the detour. But he could only stop for a few moments. So he had taken the calling card of the shop and decided to return again when he wasn't so pressed for time.

After two flights of stairs, he reached the supervisor's office and knocked. At least he still had the card to remind him where the shop was located. As the door to the office opened, Brandt reached into his lunch pail for the card and found someone else's lunch.

"Brandt," his new supervisor greeted. "How nice of you to be on time."

The sarcasm wasn't lost on Brandt, but he had bigger problems than his punctuality. He was holding someone else's lunch! There had been only two interruptions to his walk to work that morning. The pail he held had to belong to the young woman who had knocked him down.

He stepped inside the office and tried to focus on the immediate details of his job. But it was no use. Visions of a dark-haired angel filled his mind. How was he going to return the pail to her? He didn't even know her name.

two

Felicity looked down in dismay at the contents of the lunch pail on her lap. Two strawberry tarts, three dumplings, an apple, a handful of cookies, and several strands of licorice. The items reminded her more of a dessert table at one of her mother's social events than a healthy lunch. A tin cup with a balled-up napkin stuffed inside also rested at the bottom of the pail. She distinctly remembered packing a cucumber and butter sandwich, an orange, and a cup for water. She pressed her lips together, one corner turning downward as she regarded the pail again.

At least she still had the tin cup for water. And the apple would suffice in place of the orange. But the other components of this strange lunch? Well, she might enjoy one of the tarts after she finished the apple. She raised the fruit to her lips and took a bite.

"Hi, Felicity. Mind if we join you?"

"Why the long face?"

Felicity looked up as Laura and Brianna came to stand in front of her. With her mouth full, she could only nod and scoot over on the concrete wall to give them room.

Once seated, Brianna leaned close. "So I'll ask again. Why the long face?"

Felicity reached into the pail and pulled out the three dumplings, holding them up for the other two girls to see. "I bumped into someone this morning on the way to work, and somehow in the confusion our pails got mixed up. I must have ended up with his lunch."

"His?" Laura bent forward and peered around Brianna. "Did you say you bumped into a 'him'?"

She should have known. Upon their introduction that morning, the young woman with freckles spattered across her nose had made it clear she was enamored with anything that had to do with the male species. Felicity tried to think of a way to share what had happened without identifying the young man, but it was no use.

"So come on," Laura pressed. "Don't hold back with all the details. We want to know everything!"

"Correction." Brianna poked Laura with her index finger. "*You* want to know everything. I would only be interested in the basics."

"Oh, all right, Miss Priss." Laura leveled a haughty glare at Brianna. "*You* might not want to hear about this fascinating story, but *I* do." She stood and moved to the other side of Felicity, barely able to maintain her seat with the way she bounced on the wall, her eyes holding a decided gleam. Laura bit into her sandwich, then swallowed and bounced again. "Now do tell. How did it all happen?"

Felicity shook her head and laughed at the two girls who had become fast friends since that morning. It helped that she had been assigned a station nearby so they could also chat during work hours.

"You don't have to share anything with her that you don't want to share, Felicity." Brianna narrowed her eyes at Laura, who glared right back.

"Girls, please don't quarrel on my behalf." Felicity held out her hands as if to separate Brianna and Laura. "I'll be more than happy to share everything and answer any questions. Although there really isn't much to tell."

Laura folded her arms across her chest and sat back with a triumphant grin on her face. Brianna rolled her eyes and returned her attention to her own lunch, silently taking small bites of her sandwich. Felicity chuckled then took another bite of her apple, savoring the sweet juices. After swallowing, she shifted on the wall and settled back to retell her adventurous walk to work that morning.

"I was enjoying a leisurely stroll through the neighborhood until I entered the business district. About four blocks from this factory, I turned the corner and came upon five men about to start a fight."

Brianna gasped, and Laura leaned forward in anticipation.

"No one else seemed to be paying these men any mind. Only a handful of children and perhaps two or three onlookers stopped to watch."

"That's because fights happen all the time down here by the river." Brianna gave Felicity a curious look but waved her hand in dismissal. "We're lucky to have the secure fence and gate around this factory, or those fights might end up too close for comfort."

Felicity couldn't imagine living such a life on an everyday basis. But she was forced to do just that in this recent turn of events. If she let on that she was anything less than accustomed to behavior like that, her new friends might see right through her. As it was, she had to take special care with her speech and spend time studying their word choices. Her formal vernacular would be a sure sign. And she couldn't risk that.

"I agree." Felicity nodded. "I wouldn't want to encounter men like those after dark." She suppressed a shudder at the mere thought and tried to focus on something else.

"All right, so what happened after you saw the men?" Laura asked.

Felicity scrunched her eyebrows together. "It all happened so quickly; I find it difficult to recall specific details."

"Just tell us what you remember," Brianna said.

"Well, as the fight began, I couldn't tear myself away from the sight. So I remained where I stood to watch, but stayed back so I wouldn't get caught in the middle. I had just decided to leave when one of the fighters came flying in my direction and knocked me down."

"And is that when Prince Charming came to the rescue?" Laura folded her hands under her chin and batted her eyelashes.

Felicity smiled. "Not quite. When I was struck, I stumbled back a few feet from the shock and lost my footing. 'Prince Charming' as you call him is the one who broke my fall."

Laura sighed and closed her eyes. "How romantic."

Brianna reached across Felicity to poke Laura's leg, causing Laura to open her eyes.

"It's not *my* fault if you want nothing to do with the young men in town. For all we know, Felicity could have met the man of her dreams." Laura turned her attention to Felicity. "So what happened next?"

"Well, the man smacked my cheek a little and asked if I was all right. Then a few seconds later he was rushing off, saying something about being late. A young boy nearby handed a lunch pail to him, and he handed me the one he had retrieved from the ground."

"What did he look like? Was he tall? Handsome? Strong? Did he smile at you or give you his name?"

"No, no, and no." Felicity laughed at Laura's enthusiasm. If only she had taken the time to pay attention to such details. "I don't remember too much about his physical description, but as he helped me to my feet, I did have to look up at him. And since he was able to survive the impact without too much injury, I would guess he's strong."

"Oh, you're just like Brianna. You don't get the important stuff first." Laura pouted and slid off the wall to slouch against it.

Brianna exchanged an amused grin with Felicity, and they both shook their heads at Laura's antics.

"So is there any chance you'll see him again?" Brianna lifted the handle of the pail Felicity held. "I mean, you do have his lunch. You no doubt will have to figure out how to get it back to him and exchange it for yours."

Felicity hadn't really thought about that. There wasn't time to exchange names or personal information. She didn't even know where he worked. How was she going to find him again?

"Have you checked the pail?" Laura asked, as if reading her mind. "Maybe he left something in there that could identify him or help you find out where he lives."

Felicity peered inside and fished around between the tarts, dumplings, and licorice. A piece of what felt like cardboard fell between the items and against her hand. She looked closer and reached in for the card and pulled it out to read the words printed on it.

"Sam's Music," she read aloud. "Waterloo and Baldwin."

"That's what you found in his pail?" Laura peered into the pail herself then plucked the card from Felicity's hand. "Doesn't give you much to go on. But at least it's something."

The whistle sounded the end of their lunch break, and all three of them sighed.

Laura waved the card in front of Felicity's face. "So are you going to visit this music shop and see if you can find him?" She tossed it back in the pail.

"I don't know. I suppose I should, if for no other reason than I need to return his pail and get mine back."

"Right—don't even think about the possibility that he might be the prince of your dreams or anything, Miss Practical." Laura waved her hand in dismissal as she gathered her belongings and started to walk away. "Do me a favor, though.

If you make a mess of things with this guy, don't tell me about it. I only want to hear about your meeting if things go well."

Brianna stood up next to Felicity and leaned close. "Don't pay any attention to her. You do what you feel you have to do." She placed a reassuring hand on Felicity's arm. "And even if Laura doesn't want to hear about your quest to find this stranger, you can come find me."

Felicity gave Brianna an appreciative smile. "Thank you. I will be sure to tell you both what happens." She glanced at the large clock on the wall. "Now we had best get back to our stations before the supervisor marks a demerit on our time cards."

Once back at work, Felicity couldn't get her mind off the man she'd met that morning. She had managed to push him somewhat to the back of her mind up to that point, but thanks to Laura's romantic fantasies, he now occupied her thoughts full-time. What was she going to do? She had promised both Brianna and Laura that she'd do something. But the only lead she had was the card with the music shop's address on it. She couldn't exactly go waltzing up to it, hoping to find him there.

Then again, why couldn't she?

&

The same three men who had been sitting outside Sam's Music Shop were there again the next day. Brandt breathed a sigh of relief that he remembered how to get here. Without the card in the pail the young woman had, he didn't know for certain. He still remembered the nicely wrapped sandwich and orange from her lunch. Hardly enough food to serve as a snack, let alone a full meal. But he had made do and eaten a healthy portion at supper that evening. His mother had questioned his appetite and asked how he could eat everything in his pail and still be so hungry. Brandt shrugged it off, unwilling to share anything about his encounter that morning.

The next day, standing outside the music shop on a Saturday morning, the guitar and accordion melodies called to him once more.

He tipped his hat to the three men, who all nodded at him as they continued to play. For several moments he stood there and soaked in the music, allowing it to wash over him and calm his spirit. If only his father could understand the importance of music and how Brandt would love to bring it to the factories. It might help the workers' attitude if they could hear live performances like this every once in a while.

After five minutes of listening, Brandt slipped inside the store to look around. Several rows of sheet music were on display, and a handful of instruments lay in their cases. A counter separated him from the clerk, who bent over what looked like a ledger book, and behind him was a large assortment of instrument parts such as guitar strings and picks.

"Can I help you with something, sir?"

Brandt turned to see the clerk looking at him over wire-rimmed spectacles. His hair was combed to the side, and he wore an apron over his clothing.

"No, thank you," Brandt replied. "I only have a few moments before I must be off to work. So for now I'll take a look around if you don't mind."

"Not at all. My name is Matthew if you need anything."

"Thank you."

Brandt thumbed his way through several pieces of sheet music, seeing only a handful of tunes he recognized. Oh, to have the time to browse to his heart's content. But duty called, and he had to be on his way. It wouldn't be wise to be late two days in a row. At least today he had gotten an early start.

"I will have to come back another time when I can look at everything more closely." Brandt nodded to the clerk.

"You are welcome anytime." The clerk turned his attention

back to the guitar he was repairing, and Brandt slipped outside once more.

The three men sat and played a more upbeat tune, so Brandt tapped his foot to the rhythm and bobbed his shoulders in time with the beat. He turned his head to visualize the music, and from the corner of his eye he saw a young woman standing not fifteen feet away. When he pivoted to get a full glimpse of her, he almost coughed on his quick intake of breath.

It was the woman from yesterday!

Memories of their encounter and the desire to hear her polished voice once more compelled him to take a few steps in her direction. She didn't seem to notice him. Her attention was focused down the street.

Perhaps she was waiting for someone—maybe him. But she wasn't looking at the shop. So much for wishful thinking. Well, he couldn't exactly leave without at least saying something. He cleared his throat and pushed his best grin to his lips.

"So we meet again, only this time it is under more favorable circumstances."

The young woman pivoted so quickly that strands of her hair followed a second later. Her eyes widened when she saw him.

"Gracious!"

three

There it was again. That polished quality to her voice. It didn't line up with her outward appearance at all. Dressed as she was, Brandt expected a bit more brass and a bit less culture. But her choice of words, her mannerisms, and her proper posture all led him to believe there was more to her than she was allowing him to see.

He bent in a stiff and quick bow. "I am sorry for surprising you yet again. I promise it isn't how I normally introduce myself."

She tucked a few strands of her dark curls behind one ear and offered a shy smile. "There is no. . .I mean. . .it's all right. I guess I'm a little skittish."

"Don't worry about it. I'm actually glad I ran into you." He gave her a lopsided grin. "At least this time it wasn't literally."

She ducked her head and looked down at the sidewalk where they stood. Her tongue darted out to lick her lips, and then she pulled her lower lip between her teeth.

He was about to continue when she looked at him. The light green and brown of her eyes sent any coherent thought straight from his mind.

She rescued him from the awkward silence. "I know I apologized yesterday, but I want to do so again. Not only did it make you arrive even later for work, but you were forced to sacrifice your nutritious lunch and have it replaced by a cucumber and butter sandwich."

The corner of her mouth twitched, and her eyes took on a teasing light.

"Yes, but thankfully I was able to have a rather large helping at supper last night to offset my hunger." He shrugged. "At least the orange was juicy."

"The same for the apple, which, I must admit, I was surprised to find amidst the tarts, dumplings, and cookies." She gave him a penitent look. "And I'm ashamed to say I forgot to bring your pail with me. I'm told that today the food is actually brought to the workers."

She must have a job at one of the factories. How else would she know about the deal his father had made with a local vendor? "Don't worry about the pail. We can arrange the exchange another day. As for my food of choice"—Brandt held out his hands in a helpless gesture—"what can I say? I have a healthy appetite, and I need to make sure I have enough strength to do my job."

She gasped. "Oh yes, your job. Did you have any problems with being late?"

"Other than a glare from my supervisor and a brief reprimand about how many other men would love to have my job and gladly take my place, no."

He left off the part about Mr. Hathaway reminding him of the need to be professional and remain aboveboard in all aspects of his work. His supervisor was required to report on Brandt's performance to his father each week. The last thing Brandt needed was a report that cast him in a negative light. It could delay the unspecified timetable his father had established before allowing him to take over the refinery. And he was more than ready to get on with his life.

"I'm relieved to hear that. I would hate to find out that I had somehow caused you any additional issues after being the reason your day began so horribly."

"On the contrary," he countered. "Running into you was without a doubt the best thing that happened to me yesterday."

"You cannot be serious."

"But I am." He took a step to the right and pressed his shoulder against the cracked siding of the music shop's front. "I told you that I was already running late, and I just barely made it to work on time, but throughout the rest of the day I couldn't stop thinking about how we met." He winked. "Especially when I was enjoying that delicious lunch you had prepared."

A giggle escaped her lips, and she quickly covered her mouth with her hand. "At least you were able to eat your lunch in peace. I had two friends join me and spend the entire thirty minutes interrogating me about our little accident. I barely had time to eat between all the questions and answers."

"And what did you tell them?"

She pressed her lips together for a brief second. "That I had been knocked over by a young man running to work and that it took him a few minutes before he offered to help me back to my feet."

His jaw fell as his mouth opened. There was no way she had said that. Or had she? He didn't know her well enough to determine if she was joking or not, and her face didn't give away anything that would answer the question for him.

"Don't fret," she continued before he had a chance at a rebuttal. "I didn't say that. When they asked, I told them the truth." Her head tilted to the right, and she stared over his shoulder. "Of course, when I did that, it released a never-ending list of questions about you and our meeting."

Brandt crossed his arms. "The same happened to me when I told a few men at work about you."

She raised her eyebrows. "Oh really? You spoke of me with other men who work with you?"

"Only to explain why I had such an interesting lunch that day."

She giggled. "Ah, so you were forced to endure a similar situation to what I experienced."

"Yes, and it wasn't easy explaining what happened without giving the men details I couldn't provide."

A smile graced her lips. "It makes me feel better about my interrogation knowing that you had to answer questions as well."

"And I think I did a pretty good job, since I only had a vague physical description of you. I didn't even know where you were headed or how you came to be there that early in the morning."

"There wasn't exactly time for introductions."

Time. He mentally scolded himself for letting it get away from him yet again. Brandt pushed off the wall and pulled out a pocket watch from his vest. "No, and there won't be much more if we don't at least start walking." He held out his pocket watch for her to see.

She gasped and nodded. "Yes, I was almost late yesterday as well. And it was my first day. I wouldn't want to do that again. This job is too important."

"I agree." She had no idea just how important this job was for him. Everything in his life was hedging on the outcome of his performance at the factory. Then again, he had no idea what circumstances were forcing her to work, either. For all he knew, she could be in dire straits.

"So," he began as they walked side by side toward the factories. "Am I correct in assuming that you work along the river?"

"Yes. I work at the candle and soap factory."

"That isn't too far from the copper refinery where I work." In fact, it wouldn't be out of his way at all to escort her and make sure she arrived safely. This wasn't exactly a secure part of town. "We could walk together every day, if you like. Do you live nearby?"

She stumbled and nearly lost her footing. Brandt instinctively reached out to steady her.

"Are you all right?"

"Yes," she answered, sounding out of breath. "Yes, I'm fine. There must have been a crack in the sidewalk."

"All right."

"Now you asked if I live nearby." She paused and seemed to consider her words. "It isn't far away, but the woman who owns the house from where I walk is quite ill. It wouldn't be a good idea for you to come. It might do more harm than good to upset the routine."

If it wasn't good for him to come, how could it be all right for her to be there? And she didn't say she lived there, just that she walked from there. That sounded a bit odd. Brandt looked at the way she avoided his gaze and stared straight ahead. She also didn't seem willing to offer much more in the way of an explanation, so for now he'd let it be.

"Well, would you like to meet somewhere partway? I don't live too far away, either." He jerked his thumb over his shoulder. "We could meet at the music shop and go from there."

She nodded. "That would be fine."

At least she agreed to that. He didn't want to scare her off after just two meetings.

"In that case, I think it would be a good idea if we knew each other's names. If we're going to walk together, it'd be better for conversation."

She smiled and turned to look at him. "I agree."

He stopped, and she paused beside him. He extended a hand. "Brandt Dalton," he said, using his mother's maiden name, which he'd assumed for work to disguise his true identity.

She returned his handshake. "Felicity Chambers. I'm pleased to finally meet you."

❧

The trolley bells jingled on Monday morning, and a handful of passengers exchanged places on the horse-drawn conveyance at the corner of Champlain and Field. Some stepped from the platform as others climbed aboard to catch a ride. Felicity raised her hand to shield her eyes as she peered down the street in search of Brandt. He'd suggested this corner for them to meet this morning.

Had he forgotten?

She covered her mouth as a yawn escaped and blinked several times, scrunching her eyes tight to clear the sleep from them. After the blessing of sleeping later yesterday before church services, dragging herself from bed at sunrise had been nigh onto impossible. Thank goodness for Cook's strong tea. Otherwise her driver wouldn't have had the time to get her to Mrs. Gibson's early enough for her to change clothes and rush out to meet Brandt. She only swapped outfits to avoid suspicion from anyone in the Grosse Pointe district who might see her in those early morning hours. Charity work didn't normally require such common apparel. And having to change today on top of already being late made her wonder if she'd missed Brandt.

It had only been two days since they had officially introduced themselves to each other and agreed to walk together to work. On Saturday, when she had noticed the copper refinery was actually on the farthest east edge of the assembled factories, she'd protested.

"You don't have to escort me all the way to the factory, Mr. Dalton. It isn't the first time I've walked here alone."

"Nonsense," he countered. "It will be my pleasure. What kind of a friend would I be if I didn't at least make sure you arrived safely? After all, we wouldn't want you falling into another unfortunate passerby and knocking *him* off his feet."

She started to reply with the same measure of teasing but held her retort in check. Mother had reprimanded her on more than one occasion about her penchant for speaking before thinking. And she was often too forward with her remarks. Especially where men were concerned. Brandt was a new friend. She didn't need to ruin that with her untoward behavior. So she chose to dip her head in response.

"Very well. If you insist."

"I do."

"Then it appears to be settled."

After a farewell and a brief touch of his hand to his cap, they had parted ways. Brandt headed for the refinery, and she turned toward the candle and soap factory. Knowing they would walk together each morning somehow made the thought of yet another exhausting day where she came home with dried wax on her clothes and sometimes in her hair seem less daunting.

Now Monday morning had arrived, and she stood waiting for Brandt. Felicity glanced down the street again, stretching up on her tiptoes to see farther.

"Are you looking for me?"

Felicity pivoted on her heel and found Brandt standing there with his hands in his pockets and wearing a rather mischievous look on his face.

"Yes. I thought you would be coming from the other direction."

"I took a shortcut."

"By the music shop would be my guess."

He winked and sent a devilish grin her way. "You discovered my weakness. Now we don't have a choice. We must remain friends lest you spill my secret to someone else."

Felicity grinned. He sounded so much like her older brother with his quick wit and easygoing charm. But that was where the resemblance stopped.

His baggy pants were held with suspenders that hooked over his wide shoulders and pressed his cotton shirt against his chest. Scuffed and worn shoes peeked out from below the cuffs of his pants. Top that off with a cap sitting on his sandy-colored hair at a crooked angle, and he looked every bit the picture of trouble.

In fact, he reminded her of a grown-up version of little Timothy, the scrappy street urchin of Mrs. Gibson's. And just as Timothy had promised to watch out for her, Brandt did the same with his offer to walk with her to work. She couldn't imagine any two better guardians. At least if Mother inquired, she could truthfully say she wasn't walking alone.

"Is this a good meeting place for you?" Brandt asked, breaking her from her silent observation.

"It works fine."

"What direction are you coming from?"

She extended her arm to the east. "Over there."

Brandt drew his eyebrows together and frowned. "Near the Grosse Pointe district?"

Oh no! She hadn't taken the time to get her bearings before responding. She just automatically pointed toward home. She had to think of something. Quick.

"What? No. I must have gotten turned around. I meant that way." She changed from her right to her left arm and pointed to the west this time. "I come from Maple on the other side of the cemetery."

"The Elmwood or Mt. Elliott?"

"Elmwood."

Brandt seemed to accept her response as he placed his hand at her back and encouraged her to start walking toward the factory. "That's a better part of town than some, but not quite like Grosse Pointe."

She couldn't argue with him on that. The area around Maple was far different from where she really lived, but at least she hadn't chosen the poorest section of Detroit for her false address. Felicity fell in step with him and breathed a silent sigh of relief. That was close. He obviously knew the town well. She'd better be careful from now on and take a moment to make sure she didn't repeat that mistake.

"My great-grandfather is buried in Elmwood." His breath caught, and he quickly added, "Just a little wooden cross marks the grave in an out-of-the-way spot."

She couldn't be sure, but she thought she detected a trace of agitation in the latter part of his statement. But why would he sound nervous sharing about his family? Unless he was ashamed they couldn't afford more in the way of a gravestone. Felicity turned to see him swallow several times before continuing.

"He fought in the War of 1812. From the stories my father and grandfather have shared, his valiant efforts helped his unit defend the areas east of the lake region. With the New England states refusing to lend troops or financial assistance, the soldiers needed everyone they could find. So he gave it all he had."

"I have heard similar stories from my family, although I don't know too many specifics."

"After the war, he decided to move farther west with his family. My grandfather had been born while my great-grandfather was fighting. That was when they moved here to Detroit and settled. My family has been here ever since."

"Sounds like quite a legacy."

Brandt reached up and slid his thumbs under his suspenders, drawing them away from his shirt, then letting go with a snap. "Yes, we might not have many things to talk about, but we're proud of what we *have* done."

She giggled at his antics and stepped with him across Sheridan. "That's just like my family. The only story I hear repeated over and over again is how my great-grandfather was at Fort McHenry when Sir Francis Scott Key wrote 'The Star-Spangled Banner.'"

He regarded her with a tilt of his head as they walked. "Your great-grandfather fought down in Maryland? That's quite a ways from Detroit."

Felicity almost said he had been in Washington when the White House had been burned, negotiating shipping supplies for his company. But that might give her away. "Like your great-grandfather, mine didn't always live here. He was actually born in Philadelphia."

"So how did he come this far west and north?"

She shrugged as they continued on Champlain, trying to make the relocation sound less important. "He wanted a change from the life he had known as a young boy."

Leaving off the fact that he had come by way of the river in one of his company's vessels helped simplify the story. It appeared as nothing more than a vagabond young man setting off for bigger and better things. She wasn't even going to broach the topic of legacies with the connections her family had to the presidential line and other influential members of the government. No, those stories would give her away for sure.

"Detroit is a great choice, especially now that the War Between the States is over. We've seen so much improvement in industry and development, and right here in this city we have one of the best collections of factories outside of Boston. When the Sault Locks opened in the Upper Peninsula twenty years ago, they brought opportunities for everyone. It's an exciting time to live here."

The enthusiasm in his voice matched the joy on his face.

He looked like a little boy who had just been given his first piece of candy from the corner mercantile.

"I have to agree with you. Although working in the factory isn't glamorous, it provides a steady wage and gives me a sense of accomplishment."

"It's the same for me." He nodded. "Working at the refinery is hard, but I feel good at the end of the day."

He almost seemed surprised by that, but she brushed it off when he didn't say anything further.

They turned south toward Jefferson, near the river. Only a few more blocks and they would have to part ways. What could end up being a long, solitary walk would pass in no time at all. They continued in companionable silence almost to the fence surrounding the factories. Brandt paused just outside the gate.

"Do you have plans to share lunch with your friends again today?"

Now that was a question she hadn't expected to hear. "Yes, why?"

He held up her lunch pail with a sheepish grin. "Because I did my best to bring something I thought you would eat."

Laughter bubbled up from within. "Oh, gracious, I almost forgot." She dangled his pail from her fingertips. "I did the same, fresh-baked cookies and everything."

The hungry gleam in his eyes was thanks enough. She was sure Brandt would love the meal she'd brought for him. Handing him his lunch, she took hers with her other hand. Although she wanted to peek inside the folded cloth to see what he had placed in the pail, she resisted. Just in case she didn't like it, she didn't want to insult him by her expression or reaction.

"Thank you," he said with an appreciative sniff as he ran the pail under his nose. "I'm sure it'll be the best lunch I've had in a long time."

"I look forward to hearing about it tomorrow."

A crestfallen look replaced the one of anticipation on his face. "Do you not want to walk together this evening?"

She needed to get to Mrs. Gibson's as quickly as possible so she could return home in time for supper. And that meant she had to almost run to make it. She'd told Mother and Father that her work for Mrs. Gibson would require staying until five o'clock, but didn't specify it involved factory work. Mother seemed to allow for the delay and had agreed to push back the mealtime to accommodate the later arrival, but Brandt couldn't know that. "I. . .um. . .I actually take a different way home, and I wouldn't want to impose on you."

"Oh. All right." He didn't seem happy about that, but he accepted it anyway. "Then shall we meet at the corner again tomorrow?"

"Same time, same place."

"Good." He flicked the corner of his cap with his forefinger and stepped through the gate. She followed and offered a quick wave before heading for the factory. When she looked over her shoulder to see his departure, she caught him watching her, and a blush stole across her cheeks. Ducking her head, she slipped inside and out of view.

Brandt was far too charming for his own good. And if Mother knew she was keeping company with a young man of his social status? Oh my! She would forbid Felicity from continuing with this charity work. Father wouldn't be pleased, either. She only prayed she could keep it a secret.

four

Brandt took a bite of his apple then licked the juice from his lips. He walked alongside Felicity and listened as she shared about the continued illness of Mrs. Gibson. Her sacrifice for the woman was admirable. He still wondered about the specifics of her circumstances, such as what she had done before she started helping Mrs. Gibson. For now, though, he let his curiosity rest.

Felicity sighed. "I simply can't understand why her condition isn't improving. For some reason this pregnancy is taking a greater toll on her than all five of her previous ones." Frustration and pain laced her words, and a frown marred her countenance. "I am making certain to follow all the doctor's instructions, administering the proper amount of medication and seeing that she gets as much rest as possible." She sighed, brushing wisps of hair out of her eyes. "But with each passing day, there doesn't seem to be much improvement."

Brandt took another bite and pointed the apple in her direction. "At least she isn't getting worse."

Felicity cast a quick glance his way and attempted a smile. "You're right. I only wish there was something more I could do for her."

He chewed for a moment, and she fell silent beside him. "But you are no doubt helping a lot by working at the factory. The money you share is keeping her children fed. That has to be a relief to her in this time of need."

She tilted her head and pressed her lips into a thin line. A breeze stirred the loose wisps of hair at the crown of her head, and she tucked the strands she could grab behind her ear. "I suppose you're right about that. If she had to worry about food and clothing while she's sick, she would likely be far worse than she is now."

"Exactly. So don't doubt your contribution, even if her health doesn't seem to be improving." He bit the final piece of apple then tossed the core into a waste bucket outside Hardwell's Meat Market. "I have a question for you."

"Yes?"

"How did you come to know Mrs. Gibson and take a job at the factory to help her when she could no longer work?"

Felicity stumbled, and he extended a hand to steady her. The handle of her pail made a creaking sound as it swung back and forth. She regained her footing and licked her lips several times. He hoped it was a crack in the sidewalk and not his question that unsettled her. After all, he'd only asked her to share her story. Why would that cause a problem?

"Are you all right?" He kept his hand on her elbow until she'd regained her balance.

"Yes, yes." Heavy breathing accompanied her reply, but she smiled in spite of it, and he released her arm. "I'm sorry. There must have been a bit of uneven sidewalk back there."

He motioned with his head over his shoulder and chuckled. "Yeah, the sidewalk sometimes has a way of coming up to trip you when you least expect it."

A full-fledged smile accompanied his joke, and he once again felt at ease. They'd been walking together for two weeks. He wanted to see their friendship improve with each passing day—not give her a reason to withdraw.

"Back to your previous question," she said. "You asked how I came to know Mrs. Gibson."

He nodded and placed his hand at her back as they crossed Sheridan. Not a lot of activity this early in the morning, but the manners ingrained in him from childhood couldn't be ignored.

"I met her through other work I had been doing, and we struck up a fast friendship. Her little ones are quite precious, and I loved spending time with them every chance I could get."

When she didn't continue, Brandt took the opportunity to watch her. She looked away and chewed on her lower lip. He thought he saw a flash of worry cross her face, but just as quickly it was gone. He must have imagined it. A few seconds later, she resumed talking.

"When Mrs. Gibson's pregnancy forced her to give up her job at the factory, I worried about her and her family. Her husband died not long before Christmas last year from a boating accident, and she has been the one to provide for them all in his absence."

Brandt looked across the street to the left at the small grassy area the local residents considered a park. The immaculate lawns near his home made this area seem ramshackle and scraggly, but the young mother with her two playing children didn't seem to mind.

"Does she not have any other family who can help?"

"None." Felicity shook her head and frowned. "Her family didn't approve of her choice for a husband, and they disowned her." Her voice choked, but she swallowed past it. "So she was left with nothing, and when her husband died, life got even worse."

"It's hard to imagine a family being so uncaring that they'd rather leave a mother destitute than help her in her time of need."

"Not all families can bring themselves to support one of their own marrying into a lower class."

It took a moment for Felicity's words to register, but when they did, he directed his full attention on her. She avoided his eyes and increased her gait to just a little faster than his own. As he altered his pace to match hers once more, her silence gave him pause.

He wanted to believe that his own family would understand if he should choose to marry a woman who didn't abide within the same social circles. Then again, when his younger brother had almost done just that, there had been quite the uprising. And after hearing Felicity's story, there would without a doubt be problems.

His parents had yet to start arranging pairings for him, but they weren't above manipulating the circumstances to bring him together with a woman of their choosing. At a handful of events during the past few years, he had managed to avoid their attempts to force his hand. But he was twenty-three already. Mother and Father wouldn't allow his games to continue for long.

As he and Felicity turned south and headed for the river, Brandt searched for something—anything—that might get the conversation going again.

"You sound as if you speak from experience," he said. "Has someone in your family been affected by a similar circumstance as Mrs. Gibson?"

Felicity covered her sharp intake of breath with her hand and continued to avoid his gaze. "I. . .um. . . ," she stammered as her eyes darted from left to right. "I have heard stories just like Mrs. Gibson's," she finally managed. She seemed to gain confidence from that statement and continued. "In an area like this where the lives of people from different social circles can easily cross paths, it makes sense that others would find themselves facing a similar fate."

"That's a good point. We have men at the refinery from all different parts of the city. And yet they all manage to work together toward a common goal."

"You sound surprised."

Finally, she looked at him again, but this time crossness appeared in the look she gave him.

He held up his hands in mock surrender and took a step away. "I didn't mean any harm by what I said. I only meant to point out how impressed I am to see that social status doesn't seem to matter to the men who work with me. We're all there for the same reason, and we find other things in common despite where we live."

Her expression softened, and she offered a sweet smile. "I'm sorry. This situation with Mrs. Gibson hasn't been easy for me. I don't like seeing people treat others badly just because they don't live in the right place or have the right amount of money or dress a certain way."

Brandt placed a reassuring hand on her shoulder. "It's all right. I feel the same way. I run into others who don't agree, and it makes me sick to see how they treat people they believe to be inferior."

"Yes. I see how much it hurts Mrs. Gibson, and I don't want to do that to anyone."

He'd have to store that statement and pursue it at a later date. A time when he felt comfortable sharing more details about his life. For now he wanted to learn more about her.

"So what about your work at the factory? What are the other girls like who work with you?"

⁂

Felicity wasn't ready to talk about the girls she'd met, but since Brandt had shared about the refinery, it was only fair that she tell him something, too.

"It's a lot like what you describe. Do you remember the two girls I mentioned when we first met?"

He winked. "The ones who teased you about running into me in the middle of the street?"

A grin tugged at her lips. "Yes." She took his arm as they crossed Jefferson. "Brianna lives about four streets away from Mrs. Gibson's, and Laura's family is not too far from the railroad. But despite the fact that Laura doesn't have as much, they became fast friends the moment they started working together. Fortunately, they allowed me to join their little circle as well." She looked up at the cloudless blue sky and caught two sparrows engaged in a playful dance as they flew between the trees on each side of the street. "The days pass by much faster with their ongoing laughter and banter. Even the most mundane tasks seem easier with them working beside me."

Brandt grabbed a coin from his pocket and flicked it into the air before catching it again in his hand. "Sounds like you have a couple of great friends. They can be hard to find, but when you do, you don't want to lose them."

The melancholic quality to his voice momentarily distracted Felicity. But Brandt didn't seem to want to share anything more about his remark, so she let it go.

"I never imagined I would enjoy working at the factory as much as I do. The supervisors keep us moving at a grueling pace, but we all manage to make it through a day. It's not only a blessing to know that I am helping Mrs. Gibson, but it gives me confidence in my own abilities as well."

Brandt furrowed his brow for a moment, and she returned his questioning gaze. He waved his hands and dismissed what he had obviously been about to say, and Felicity shrugged. Perhaps it wasn't important or he was going to ask her later.

She sighed. "But it always surprises me to see how young some of the girls are who work in a factory."

"We have young boys in the refinery, too. Some of them are needed because of their small hands and ability to get in between the machines. Of course, this also means there is a higher risk of them losing a finger or suffering a greater injury as a result."

Felicity closed her eyes at that thought. Little Timothy came to mind, and she cringed at the idea of telling Lucy her son had been hurt on a machine similar to the ones Brandt described simply to keep the refinery running with smooth precision. Then again, Timothy didn't work at the refinery or anywhere near the river district. He ran errands for the local grocer and delivered food to those who couldn't get out on their own. For now he was safe.

"We have an area that uses machines like that," she continued. "But most of the work I do involves the shaping of candles and carving of soap after the other girls make the wax molds and combine the lye with the oils."

Felicity stopped in front of a window where the merchant inside replaced several wooden toys with newer ones. Brandt paused with her as they looked through the window to see a train with seven cars attached. A red rubber ball sat next to jacks that shimmered in the early morning sunlight, and she noticed what looked like a cup on a stick with a ball attached to a string. She wasn't sure what a child would do with that toy, but the merchant seemed proud to have it on display. He acknowledged them with a nod and a wave; then he disappeared farther into the store. Felicity turned and continued walking.

"There is a little girl, though, who isn't much more than eleven or twelve. Her name is Julia, and I met her last week. When I asked her about how she came to work at the factory, she said her family needed the money. With her father injured and her mother having to take care of three younger children, she was the logical choice."

Brandt sighed. "That happens a lot, I'm afraid. Several boys at the refinery are in the same situation."

Felicity placed a hand on Brandt's arm and turned to face

him. "But that's not all. Julia went on to tell me how grateful she is that God blessed her with strong arms and legs so that she *can* go to work for her family." She pivoted and started walking again. "I was amazed at the faith she had at such a young age. You would think she might blame God for letting her father get injured or making it so that she was the oldest and didn't have a brother old enough to work in her place."

"It seems as if she's accepted her duty and found a way to be happy in spite of it."

"I could learn a lot from her."

"It's sad that she is forced to work at a young age, but you're not too different."

She scrunched her eyebrows together. "What do you mean?"

"Well, you didn't *have* to share your wages with Mrs. Gibson, but you chose to help her. I daresay little Julia wasn't given that option. She's helping her family, just like you. Still she smiles. And despite Mrs. Gibson's illness, you focus on the good things about your work for her rather than dwelling on the problems."

"When you put it that way, I can see what you mean." She hadn't even thought to compare herself to Julia, but Brandt was able to make a solid parallel. "I at least have my older brother to help, so I'm not solely responsible like Julia."

Brandt again flipped the coin he held into the air. "God has an uncanny way of helping us turn what we don't think we want into something we do."

Brandt must have some measure of faith as well. His self-assured delivery told Felicity as much. She believed her own to be steady, but at times she struggled with doubt. Knowing Brandt shared that faith and seeing how little Julia lived out her own each day made Felicity happy to be in such good company.

She tilted her head. "And if we stop protesting, we might

be able to see the good."

"Right." Brandt pushed open the gate to the factories and held it as Felicity walked in front of him.

"It seems the time has come for us to part ways again. But I'll see you tomorrow?"

Brandt nodded. "Same time. Same place. I'll be there."

She headed to work, pleased to know she could count on him to walk with her. If only her future were so clear and certain.

five

Brandt ascended the front steps of his home after work and reached for the brass latch just as the wide oak door swung open before him. The composed and dispassionate face of his butler, Jeffrey, welcomed him from the doorway. Every hair was in place, and every crease in his uniform ironed sharply. How Jeffrey managed to maintain such a crisp appearance all day never ceased to amaze him, especially when Brandt would wrinkle his clothing before even setting one foot outside.

"Good evening, sir." The stalwart man dipped his head in his customary greeting, never once breaking his rigid stance. "Your father has requested to speak with you as soon as you are settled."

Brandt stepped into the entryway. The polished wooden floors gleamed in the waning evening sun. He closed his eyes for a brief moment. Just what he didn't want the second he walked in the door. Perhaps he could stall for a bit.

He opened his eyes and looked at the butler. "Thank you, Jeffrey. Shall I find him in his study?"

"Yes, sir." The man didn't flinch. "And Cook has asked me to inform you that supper is to be served on schedule."

Brandt raised his eyebrow at Jeffrey. "On schedule? Is Cook in a good mood this evening?"

The barest hint of a grin tugging at Jeffrey's lips caused an answering one to pull at Brandt's.

"Never mind that, Jeffrey. I suppose I should be grateful and not jest. Otherwise I might find myself going without food entirely the next time."

"That seems to be the wise choice, sir."

No matter how hard he tried, Brandt had never been able to break Jeffrey of his unemotional state. Tonight obviously wouldn't be any different. So he handed his lunch pail and cap to the butler. With a shake of his head, he turned toward the broad staircase. It rose from the expansive entryway and curved around to the right as it connected to the second floor. His father could wait a few moments.

As he took the stairs two at a time, he turned to look over his shoulder to where Jeffrey walked toward the kitchen, head held high and lips pressed into a firm line. There had been times when the butler had allowed a brief smile or glint in his eyes to slip almost unnoticed. But Brandt always caught it. Somewhere deep down was a man with a diabolical sense of humor waiting to get out. He wondered if he'd be there to see it when Jeffrey let loose.

"Good evening, Sarah." Brandt dipped his chin and acknowledged one of the newer maids his mother had hired as she passed him in the wide hallway.

She bobbed a quick curtsy midstride and continued on her way without a word.

Brandt walked toward his private room. The carpet on the floor absorbed the sounds of his footsteps as he turned the polished knob and stepped inside. The scent of cinnamon and cloves greeted him, no doubt from the potpourri set out by Sarah not long ago. A pleasant breeze stirred the gauzy curtains on the far side of the room.

For a brief moment he entertained the thought of flopping across the soft mattress of his four-poster bed. But he might fall asleep, and that would anger his father. So instead he headed toward the window and brushed back the flimsy material. Leaning against the frame, he placed a fist on his hip and looked down at the street below.

Well-dressed men and women, young ladies and gentlemen, all ventured to and fro on their way to their respective destinations. He contrasted their polished appearances with the men who worked side by side with him and the young ladies Felicity described from the factory.

Uncomplicated and simple.

They no doubt never worried about how they would dress for supper or how to bow properly when addressing certain members of society or which form of address was required at social functions when greeting their hosts. No, they went about their days unhindered by the confines of social customs. Just once Brandt wished he could be that free.

For the time being, he had a glimpse of that life while working at the refinery. Beneath it all remained the truth that he would one day assume control of the place where he worked. And when that time came, his adventures among the common classes would be over.

A knock on his door made Brandt turn to see Sarah standing in the hall, her head down.

"Yes? What is it, Sarah?"

"Your father has sent me to fetch you, sir," she answered in a low tone, her words barely distinguishable.

Brandt released a heavy sigh and crossed the width of his room. "I do suppose I have kept him waiting long enough." He started to follow Sarah then looked down at his attire. "Uh, do allow me a moment to change first. Our talk will no doubt take us right up to supper, and I don't wish to appear at the table dressed as I am."

A tinge of pink stained Sarah's cheeks, but she continued to avoid his gaze. She only dipped another curtsy and nodded, stepping back to allow him to close the door.

Her youthful innocence brought Felicity's face to mind. Perhaps he could recommend that his mother hire her as a maid in place of her work at the factory. No. That would no doubt cause them both discomfort. Not only that, but she'd find out the type of life he led. That wouldn't work at all.

Brandt kicked off his shoes and quickly swapped the rough work shirt, suspenders, and pants with a crisp cotton top and pressed slacks from his cherrywood wardrobe. He donned freshly shined shoes and a dinner jacket to please Mother, and he once again moved toward the door.

When he opened it, Sarah stood waiting on the other side. Father had no doubt left explicit instructions for her to personally escort him downstairs. Far be it from him to cause one of their servants to disobey orders. With a nod at the young girl, he clicked his door shut and followed her until she left him standing at the doorway to his father's study.

"I was wondering when you would get around to joining me, son. I thought perhaps you had gotten lost again."

The poor attempt at a joke wasn't lost on Brandt.

"No, sir, I merely wanted to change out of the clothes I wore to the factory."

Every time he was late for a meeting or delayed his response to come when called, Father made some remark about getting lost. Brushing it aside, Brandt stepped into the darkened room.

Every bit of it fairly shouted his father's affluence. From the dusted bookshelves teeming with old and new books, to the oversized mahogany desk that sat in the middle of the room, to the oriental carpet that covered most of the floor. The imposing yet simple decorations fit the patriarch of the Lawson family, Devon Montgomery Lawson, to a T. Not a thing was out of place. Not a paper out of order.

"I applaud your foresight, son." He leaned down and struck a match on the hardwood floor and lit his pipe, then inserted the wooden piece into his mouth. Gesturing toward the Queen Anne chair opposite, he invited Brandt to sit.

"Was there something of import you wished to discuss, sir?" Brandt flipped up the edge of his jacket as he took his seat.

"Hmm?" His father mumbled around the pipe then removed it from his lips to hold it aloft. "Oh yes. It has been at least a week since we have spoken about your progress at the refinery. I wanted to inquire about your work there and your thoughts on how the entire operation is run."

"Well, sir, Mr. Sanderson runs a fairly tight order of operations. There isn't a lot that happens where he isn't aware of it."

"Ah yes. Bartholomew. He is one of the best men I have among the supervisors and management staff."

Brandt started to settle back into his chair, but at the disapproving glance from his father, he straightened. "His meticulous attention to detail can be both a benefit and a hindrance."

"How so?"

"Take the operating of the machines, powered by the water from the river. When something breaks or gets lodged somewhere inside, it can shut down that part of the refinery until it gets fixed, which can interrupt the production schedule."

"Go on." Father took another puff of the pipe.

"Since Mr. Sanderson seems to be everywhere at once, when a problem arises, he immediately has someone on hand to perform the repairs."

"As well he should. So tell me how it can be a hindrance."

Brandt leaned forward and placed his palms on the edge of the desk. "His presence can be intimidating to some of the workers, sir. They sometimes spend more time worrying about where Mr. Sanderson is than they do on their productivity levels."

His father pounded a fist on the desk, rattling the glass inkwell with a pen inside. "Then perhaps those men should find other means of employment. If they can't keep their minds on their work, they might not be the best men for the job."

He extended one hand toward his father, palm upward. "But that's not what I meant, sir."

"Then pray tell, do explain, for I am not following your line of reasoning."

"The men who work beside me are good men. Hardworking and devoted to their jobs. But I'm sure you can see how disconcerting it can be to have your supervisor seemingly looking over your shoulder at every turn. You can't help but wonder if you're doing a satisfactory job or if he is finding fault with your performance and you might soon be told you're no longer needed."

The truth of Brandt's assessment seemed to dawn on his father. The man took a few puffs of his pipe and stared over Brandt's shoulder at the paneled wall behind him. Several long moments passed in silence. Brandt didn't want to report anything that might jeopardize anyone's job. But Father had asked him to be honest about the working conditions and assess them from the perspective of a common worker, not a supervisor. That's exactly what he was doing.

"So," his father began, "you feel that the productivity levels will increase if Bart were to become a little less conspicuous and only appear when his presence is required?"

Brandt nodded. "I do believe that will help the workers to relax and allow them to breathe easier, sir. Yes."

"Allow me a day or two to mull over this further, and I'll speak with you again two days hence."

"Fair enough, sir."

"Now what of the young lady you encountered at the beginning of your work assignment?"

Brandt's eyes widened. How did Father know about Felicity? He hadn't said a word to anyone here at the house, other than Cook when he had asked her to prepare that special lunch last week. And she had promised not to tell a soul.

"Don't act so surprised, son. I am not without my own network of information, provided the need arises."

The smug expression on his father's face didn't help matters any. He had hoped to avoid this conversation for a little while longer. Just until he was more certain about Felicity. But he couldn't get out of this now. He had to give his father some kind of answer.

"She works in the soap and candle factory at the other end of the yard. We had an unfortunate encounter on our respective first days of work, and to apologize for my haste, I offered to walk with her and see her safely to work."

All right, so he had minimized the significance of their friendship. At least he hadn't lied.

"And does this young lady have a name?"

Brandt hesitated. Should he give his father that type of information? The man had just told him about the extensive resources he had at his disposal. Then again, what harm could come of providing a name?

"Felicity Chambers, sir."

"And you walk with her to work?"

"When our paths cross. Yes, sir." His father didn't need to know that they purposefully planned for their paths to meet every morning.

"Based upon the care you took in preparing lunch for her that one morning when you had to return her lunch pail, I suspect she has become more than an acquaintance you happened to meet on the road."

Brandt didn't say a word. He might reveal the truth of his feelings and convey to his father more than he wanted the man to know. He already seemed to know more than enough. No sense in adding to what he had discovered through other means.

"Your silence says more than words, my son. If she works at the factory, her status is not equal to yours, and I caution you to remember that. We cannot afford another situation like what happened with your younger brother when he attempted to steal away for a rendezvous with that waif he met near the park."

Now why did Father have to go and bring up that story? Brandt rolled his eyes. It had happened more than two years ago, and it had only lasted long enough for tongues to wag for a few days before everyone forgot about it and went about their business. His time spent with Felicity was nothing like that. She had more refinement than dozens of other ladies he knew. And to see her compared to the girl his brother had met made his ire rise.

"I assure you, Father," he began, keeping his temper in check, "you will not see a repeat of those circumstances. Felicity and I merely enjoy a conversation to break up the silence of the walk. When we cross paths, it helps pass the time on the way to the river."

"Conversation? That is all?" His father quirked an eyebrow and regarded Brandt with a wary expression.

"Nothing more, sir. I assure you."

His father inhaled deeply and stood. "Very well. I shall take you at your word, for now. But should anything change, be aware that I will find out about it."

Of course he would. His father kept a close eye on everything Brandt did. At times he felt like the workers under Mr. Sanderson's watch. Then he remembered that everything his father did, he did to prepare him for the responsibility of managing and owning the refinery and other factories. Once he assumed that position, his life would be under even tighter scrutiny. He couldn't afford any mistakes now, let alone after he was placed in charge.

"I understand, sir." Brandt placed his hands on the arms of his chair and pushed himself to his feet. "And I assure you, you have no reason for concern."

"All right. Now let's make our way to the dining room. From the smells coming down the hall, I believe we're having a roast this evening."

Brandt chuckled a little and relaxed. Despite his over-bearing and somewhat intrusive nature, his father wasn't all bad. He handled things the only way he knew how. With direct bluntness. Better that than deception. At least Brandt always knew where he stood.

Now if only he could figure out Felicity.

☙

"What do you have for lunch today?"

Felicity peered around Brandt's shoulder and tried to sneak a peek at his lunch pail, but he held it away from her, out of arm's reach.

"Much of the same. Why?"

Well, the contents of his lunch seemed to speak of a different social class, but she didn't want to share those concerns with him. So she shrugged. "No reason. I merely wondered if you had decided to actually assemble a small measure of substance rather than the substantial amount of sweets you normally include."

Brandt quirked one eyebrow and leveled a smirk in her direction. "Are you saying you believe I'm less than the image of perfect health?" He stopped in the middle of the sidewalk then struck a pose with his chin held high, sticking out his chest in an abnormal fashion.

Felicity covered her mouth and giggled. "Well, you do have

to admit the lunches I've seen have weighed rather heavily on the cookies and sweets side. It's difficult to imagine how you remain uninfluenced by the sheer levels of sugared items you consume."

Brandt tilted his head and regarded her with a puzzled expression. He relaxed his stance. The look on his face was a mixture of curiosity and uncertainty, as if he weighed her against some unknown standard. Felicity wasn't sure if she would wind up on the positive end of the scale or the negative.

"Is something the matter?" she asked.

"What?" He shook his head as if pulling himself from a trance.

"I asked if something was the matter. You're staring at me in an unusual manner."

"Oh, it's nothing." Brandt waved his hands in front of him in scissorlike fashion. "For a moment, I thought. . ."

"What?"

"No. It's not important."

She had a hard time believing that. If it wasn't important, why would it cause him to stare? And why would he be regarding her in such an odd way? But she couldn't force him to answer. If he wanted to tell her, he would.

The only thing that came to mind was her choice of words. He hadn't seemed to be bothered by that before. Even so, she should be more careful.

"You mentioned the other day that you had been late getting home after work. Did you make anyone else in your family upset because they had to wait for you?"

"No." He started walking again. "In fact, last night I was early. And I ended up having a talk with my father."

"Oh? About what?"

He stared straight ahead as they continued toward the river. Normally he would glance in her direction a few times as he spoke. Today he didn't. Perhaps that conversation was the reason for his behavior shift.

"Work, the refinery, how I'm liking my job, the men who work with me. Typical conversation topics where my father is concerned."

"At least he sounds like he supports you."

"He does do that. But he can try my patience, too."

"How so?"

"In some of his expectations and how he thinks there's only one way to do things. Once in a while he'll warn me about something when I know there's no reason for concern."

Brandt seemed to be rather vague this morning. Like he was dancing around the specifics instead of coming right out and saying what was on his mind. His father must have said something to bring about this change. And the difference she noticed wasn't just in what he said. It was in the way he looked at her and how distant he acted compared to the camaraderie they'd shared up to this point.

"Did you talk about a specific situation where he felt you needed to be careful?"

"Uh, no."

His answer came just a second after her question. And he again avoided her gaze. Something was definitely different.

"I'm sure he's only looking out for you. Like all fathers do."

"I suppose."

He fell into silence and didn't seem too interested in continuing the conversation. Felicity regarded him with a sideways glance as she matched her stride to his. He remained introspective and not forthcoming with much detail. Every man deserved to keep his thoughts close, but this didn't feel right. Something kept him distant, and she didn't like this side of him. She hoped this phase wouldn't last long.

six

"Felicity, dear, would you be so kind as to slip into the kitchen and see where Rebecca stands on preparations for the party?"

"Yes, Mother."

This task normally fell on Mother's shoulders, as she had a way with Rebecca. But this time it was Felicity's turn. Mother and Rebecca were a lot alike. Somehow they managed to maintain their civility and respect for one another, despite their equal penchant for perfection. Felicity knew everything would be in order. It was pointless to go check on Rebecca. She tried to keep her shoulders from slumping, but Mother noticed.

"Felicity." The warning tone made Felicity stop in her tracks.

"Yes, Mother?" She turned. *Here it comes.*

"We've had this conversation many times. It is high time you learn how to run a household. It won't be long until you marry and take charge of your own staff and servants. You need to be assertive and authoritative, showing confidence, not uncertainty or hesitation."

Felicity had heard the speech so often she had almost committed it to memory. Mother was many things, and repetitive held the top spot on the list. But Rebecca didn't need a watchdog. This task was pointless.

"I only remind you because I wish for both my daughters to receive the proper instruction and education in all areas of womanhood. It would simply not do if I sent you off on your own without adequately preparing you for what may come. And I don't wish to fail you as a mother."

On the contrary, it was more likely the desire to maintain control over everyone in her home that drove her. But Felicity wouldn't dare verbalize that thought.

"I know, Mother, and we thank you for your attention to detail." She lowered her chin a little. "I apologize for my poor behavior. Please forgive me."

"Apology is accepted. Now off with you. We have less than two hours before the garden party. Everything must be perfect."

Felicity headed for the kitchen, pushing open the swinging door and slipping inside before it had a chance to spring back and smack her.

Rebecca clenched a wooden spoon in her left fist and shoved her right hand against her slender hip as she spoke.

"Now how many times do I have to tell you? I'm working hard to get this menu finished for Mrs. Chambers, and—" She paused. Immediate remorse crossed her face, and she relaxed her reprimanding pose. "Oh, Miss Felicity. I didn't know it was you. I thought it was Martin again asking when the noontime meal would be ready."

That sounded just like their butler. Always thinking about food, no matter how recently he'd eaten. It could be thirty minutes after breakfast, and his mind would be on the midday meal. But Rebecca was another matter. Most women who worked in the kitchens of the families living nearby boasted a girth to match their obvious love of food. Not so with their cook. Her shapely form was the envy of all the other cooks on the avenue.

Felicity smiled. "It's all right, Rebecca. It's only me. Mother is otherwise occupied with matters pertaining to the garden party. She asked me to come and inquire about the progress you're making." With a reassuring hand on Rebecca's arm, she added a light squeeze. "As if I even need to check."

Rebecca relaxed and returned the smile. "Child, you are going to go quite far with an attitude like that. It's a real pleasure working here, knowing that I get to see your shining face." She wagged her index finger at Felicity. "I don't let too many people in my kitchen. But you are always the exception."

Felicity leaned in close, peering in both directions before meeting Rebecca's eyes. "Don't worry. I promise not to tell anyone. It'll be our little secret."

The woman straightened with a nod. "Good. See that it stays that way." She winked then pivoted toward the sideboards along the east wall. "Now let me show you what I've finished so far from your mother's menu." She grinned and winked again. "Because you and I both know she'll expect a detailed report. Here." She handed several pieces of paper to Felicity. "As I name each item, you can cross it off on the list."

Felicity stepped with Rebecca down the line of delectable items that had been prepared, drawing a line through each name as it was called. The cook had always been her favorite staff member. She had embraced Felicity's interest in cooking with enthusiasm, touting the little girl as a prodigy in the culinary arts. The cook and her husband had no children of their own, but Rebecca said Felicity brought her enough joy to make up for a dozen children.

But enough living in the past. Mother had a garden party to host. If Felicity dallied too long with Rebecca, Mother would grow suspicious and come investigate. Better to assemble the facts for a report and beat a hasty retreat from the kitchen.

"It seems you have everything under control. . .as usual." She winked at Rebecca. "I believe Mother is now outside. I'll venture out to the veranda and provide the update. Perhaps then she'll stop fretting over the food being ready in time."

"Oh, it will be," Rebecca vowed. "This isn't the first garden party your mother has hosted."

"Nor will it be the last, I'm certain." With a final brush of Rebecca's arm, Felicity slipped outside.

⁊

"So did you hear that Aimee Parker has been seen on the arm of Jonathan Hancock for nearly three weeks straight?"

"Really?" Angela's voice raised an octave. "How exciting! Who told you this?" She sat perched on the edge of her seat.

Rachel ticked off the path the news had taken, spread from one woman to the next. "Widow Callahan told Mrs. Wipple, who in turn told my mother, who then told me."

"Do you think this means we'll be hearing a betrothal announcement soon? I have the perfect idea for staging a celebration for Aimee if that's the case."

Betrothals, engagements, romantic entanglements. One of these days, it might be Felicity's turn to have one. Her mind drifted to thoughts of Brandt. In all their conversations he had never once mentioned a young lady's name. That didn't necessarily mean he didn't have a special person in his life. It also didn't mean he did. Sure, he'd been a bit distant the last time they spoke, and he seemed to avoid answering her questions with direct answers. Up to that point, though, he'd been attentive and quite the gentleman, expressing interest in her and what she had to say. If she didn't know better, she might think he was interested in her. But that was impossible.

Felicity sipped her tea and listened to the banter volley back and forth between her two friends. They reminded her of Brianna and Laura from the factory. Amazing how the two sets of girls seemed so similar, despite their respective social standings. Even more remarkable that she had found friends at the factory to help ease the loss of her best friends here in her familiar world.

"What about you, Felicity?"

"Yes, is there a young man who has caught your eye recently?"

Felicity blinked and started. She placed her teacup on the saucer and looked back and forth between Rachel and Angela. She had been trying to pay attention. How could she have lost track of the conversation that fast?

"I'm sorry. Would you mind repeating the question?"

The two exchanged a knowing look, grins turning their lips upward at the corners. Rachel spoke first.

"We want to know if any of the young gentlemen have caught your eye."

Angela ran her tongue over her teeth. The ever-present twinkle in her eyes brightened. "By the way we caught you daydreaming, it's clear what the answer will be."

The image of Brandt again popped into Felicity's mind, and she tried to dislodge it. There was no way she was going to tell these two about him. They wouldn't allow her a moment's peace until every morsel of information was revealed. There might come a day when that disclosure would be unavoidable, but for now she'd do everything she could to keep it at bay.

"As you both well know, there are several handsome and eligible men who have caught the eye of nearly every young woman we know."

"That isn't what we asked, Felicity, and you know it." Rachel pressed her lips into a thin line. "Now answer the question, or I'll have Angela devise an alternative method of getting what we want."

Rachel wasn't one to jest, so Felicity knew she'd better think fast. She sighed. Forcing nonchalance, she raised her shoulders about an inch and shook her head. "As of right now, there are no young men we know who have captured my attention." Her friends were about to protest, but she cut them off before they had a chance to form any words. "However, there may be one who has displayed a great deal of potential in the field of suitors."

They didn't need to know that the man to whom she referred was Brandt.

"Aha!" Rachel nearly upset her teacup when she sat up straighter. A handful of matrons cast disparaging looks in their direction, so she ducked her head and lowered her voice. "I knew you weren't withdrawing from the race."

"Race?" Angela asked.

"Yes, Angela," Rachel answered with a touch of impatience. "The race in finding a young man worthy of our affections so that he might become so enamored he will offer a proposal of marriage in an instant."

Felicity and Angela covered their mouths and laughed behind their hands. Rachel had just attracted the attention of the dowager women. They didn't need to do it again. And Mother had made remarks about Rachel's influence not being the best for Felicity. If word got back to her that they were being less than appropriate at this little garden party, Mother might forbid all association. That would be the worst thing that could happen.

"I'm surprised that your mother hasn't already been speaking with some of her friends about arranging a match for you, Rachel." Felicity tucked her chin a little toward her chest and leveled a glance at her friend. If she had been wearing eyeglasses, she would have been staring over the top of the rims. "Didn't she mention at one point that she didn't trust your judgment when it came to selecting the proper husband?"

Angela gasped. "Did your mother truly say that?"

Rachel rolled her eyes and raised her teacup with calm assurance. "The only reason Mother made that statement was because she happened to see me making eyes at Benjamin Bradford one time. She doesn't understand that despite his mischievous nature, he's a fine gentleman when the situation warrants it."

Felicity exchanged a knowing look with Angela, who smiled and nodded. "And I suppose you've been in such a situation with Benjamin where you've had the opportunity to witness this upstanding behavior?"

Pink stained Rachel's cheeks, and the young woman averted her gaze. She was normally unaffected by good-natured jabs. That telltale reaction said more than any words might.

"I thought this conversation was supposed to be about potential suitors *you* have in mind, Felicity. How did we get around to discussing my preferences?"

No matter what, Rachel always managed to steer the topic of discussion back where she wanted it.

"Isn't anyone interested in inquiring about *my* standing where beaux are concerned?"

Rachel waved off Angela's question with a simultaneous blend of indifference and yearning. "Oh, everyone knows you'll end up marrying Nicholas Kennedy. You two have been paired since birth. There's no way you're going to get out of that arranged match."

"And not likely either of you will protest." Felicity winked, and Angela grinned.

"It's true." Angela placed one hand on her chest and struck a dramatic pose, her facial features softening into a daydreaming state. "Nicholas and I have come to an understanding where our parents are concerned."

"Don't you mean, neither one of you is able to defy their edicts over your lives?" Rachel interjected.

"No." Angela straightened, indignation replacing the

softness from a moment ago. "We simply have no desire to go against their wishes." Her chin thrust upward, and her eyes formed mere slits. "Nicholas and I are perfectly happy to continue with the plans that have been laid. Were we not in agreement, the circumstances would be quite different. But neither Nicholas nor I have any reason to challenge what we believe is a good match."

"Well, I think it's wonderful that the two of you have developed a fondness for each other in spite of the match-making schemes." Felicity caught Rachel's eye and silently advised her to let that particular topic rest. "Mother hasn't ventured into that territory in recent weeks, but I know it's on her mind. After all, we *are* approaching our twentieth year. Most other young ladies we know are married or engaged already. It won't be long before we're all married and starting families of our own."

"Yes," Rachel agreed with a nod, "but that time isn't here yet. So for now let's enjoy our time together while we have it."

Felicity allowed her friends to shift back into talk of other young women they knew or the latest faux pas committed at a garden party or cotillion. Brandt had popped into her mind at the mere mention of a beau. True, they'd been walking together for a month now and he'd been in her thoughts a lot lately, but that didn't mean anything. Did it?

Somehow, despite every attempt Felicity made to avoid it, Brandt had managed to sneak his way into the mental image she created each time she pondered her future. Where the picture she envisioned used to include two or three young men from fine, upstanding families, now it featured Brandt standing side by side with the other gentlemen. And when each one was compared against the other, Brandt always came out on the winning end.

That both concerned and excited her at the same time.

To think that a common man like Brandt might be able to compete with the men who traveled in her social circles and come out the champion. It was too much to even imagine possible. So for now that prospect would remain in her dreams.

seven

Felicity ran a cool, damp cloth over Lucy's face.

"Now, Mrs. Gibson, you make certain you don't overtax yourself."

"I promise," came the weak response.

A hint of color had returned yesterday, and this evening the light in Lucy's eyes brightened the dull expression she'd been wearing of late. Felicity had worried that Mrs. Gibson's health had only continued to decline the past three months. But for the first time in weeks she showed signs of improvement. That alone gave Felicity hope and confidence in her service.

"I've put some chicken broth on the stove, and Marianne has the rest of your supper under control." Felicity reached for the handles of her carpetbag and turned toward the small room off the main one. "I must say," she continued as she glanced over her shoulder, "it is truly wonderful to see the spark back in your eyes."

Lucy offered a wan smile. "It is all thanks to you, my dear. And Marianne." Her voice lacked volume, but it was clear and strong. "You both have been true angels. I know God will reward you for your selfless help." She caressed her swollen abdomen. "I pray this little one will have the pleasure of meeting you and knowing such a beautiful young woman."

Felicity paused a moment. She hadn't thought about what she'd be doing once Lucy was back on her feet again. Mother would likely help her find another family in need of assistance, but it would be nice to be able to come back and visit. Lucy was just now reaching her eighth month, so she still had several weeks before that time came. For now, Lucy needed reassurance.

"That child of yours will be strong and healthy, as long as you continue to follow the doctor's instructions. Just wait and see." She placed her hand on the knob and opened the door to the other room. "Now I must change, lest I be late getting home this evening. Mother and Father already eat later than normal. I don't need to give them further concern."

Felicity swapped the coarse clothing for her fine silk walking dress in record time. The material almost felt foreign to her. These days she spent more time in the plain outfits than the tailored fabrics from her seamstress. She was a completely different person when dressed in such a simple fashion. If Mother ever saw her, the proud matriarch would suffer from a case of the vapors.

Mother! Felicity ceased her ruminations and shoved the working clothes into her carpetbag. With a hasty farewell she rushed from the Gibson home and headed toward the corner where she met her driver to take her to her family's town house on Belvidere in the Grosse Pointe district.

Sneaking in the rear door through the room next to the kitchen, Felicity peered around the corner to see Rebecca turned away from her. She tiptoed toward the back stairs and cringed when the bottom step creaked.

"If you insist upon attempting to slip into this house unnoticed, you might consider hanging a rope from your bedchamber window or using the tree branches to the rear of the house."

With her lower lip between her teeth, Felicity turned to face her cook. The woman's flaxen hair was wound into a tight bun with a few flyaway strands framing her face. A raised eyebrow mixed with the scolding tone made Felicity feel like a little girl instead of a nineteen-year-old young woman.

"I am sorry, Rebecca. But I don't wish Mother to take notice that I am late yet again. And if I used the front door, Martin would announce my tardiness." She pleaded with her eyes. "Promise you won't breathe a word to anyone?"

Rebecca pursed her lips and mimicked a chastising expression Felicity's mother often used. "All right. But there will come a time when I will no longer be able to conceal your activities. And be forewarned." The cook wagged her index finger in Felicity's direction. "I overheard your mother and father mentioning your charity work earlier this afternoon. They will no doubt wish to speak with you before supper."

Felicity's heart stopped for a second, and the blood drained from her face. Talk about her charity work? If Mother and Father together had discussed this, the result of that conversation wouldn't be good. Rebecca didn't need to see her worry, though, so Felicity forced a smile to her face.

"Thank you, Rebecca. You're a true kindred spirit."

The cook cleared her throat with a grunt and returned to her duties. Felicity spun around toward the stairs again and hastened to the second level. With a glance to the left and right, she verified the absence of any other household members then slipped toward the east wing and her private room. Just as she stowed the carpetbag behind some of her gowns in the wardrobe, a knock sounded on her door.

"Come in!"

The knob turned, and the door opened just a few inches. Her fourteen-year-old sister, Cecily, peered around the edge then bounded into the room and plopped on Felicity's bed, her carefully styled blond curls bouncing with the action.

"It's about time you came home. Father just arrived, and Mother sent me to fetch you. They're waiting in the parlor."

She gave Felicity a mischievous grin. "Did you do something to upset them again?"

Felicity placed her hands on her hips and pursed her lips. "I'm sure I have no idea what you're talking about. Rebecca informed me that Mother and Father simply wish to discuss my charity work." And she prayed the end result of the conversation wouldn't put an end to that work. She wagged a playful finger at Cecily. "I'm sorry to disappoint you, but I doubt you'll find any fodder for your incessant torment." She forced a sweet smile to hide her inner turmoil. "Thank you for coming to notify me, though."

"Well, you'd better come tell me the moment you're done talking. I want to hear all the details."

Felicity shook her head. "I'm sure you'll find out everything one way or another. Whether it be from me or Father." She turned toward her dressing table. "Now I'm going to take just a moment to powder my nose and then report to the parlor immediately."

Cecily climbed off the bed. "Very well. I know when I'm not wanted." She headed back toward the door to the hall. "I will tell Mother and Father you will be down straightaway."

As soon as the door closed, Felicity breathed a sigh of relief. From the moment she heard the knock, her heart had been in her throat. That was too close. Just one minute longer and she might have crossed paths with Father. She normally made it home a full thirty minutes before him. There would have been no end to the questions had they arrived at the same time.

After a quick glance in the looking glass, she left her room and headed downstairs. If Mother didn't even want to wait for Father to relax after arriving home, Felicity had better not delay her appearance.

The soft murmur of voices traveled into the entryway as

soon as Felicity stepped off the stairs. She sent a silent prayer heavenward that whatever her parents had to say, it wouldn't put an end to her daily work. Before she moved into the doorway, she took a deep breath and willed her heart to beat at a normal rhythm.

"Do stop dawdling in the hallway, Felicity dear, and please join us."

Her mother's voice carried across the room and beckoned Felicity to obey. At least she didn't sound upset. A trifle impatient, perhaps, but cordial overall.

Felicity walked toward her parents and attempted to gauge their thoughts by the expressions they wore. Mother perched on the settee with her hands folded in her lap and her long legs tucked underneath, her lips pressed into a nondescript line. Father towered behind one of the wingback chairs, his fingers curled around the wood frame above the cushioned back. His face held no indication of his thoughts. When neither of them spoke, she swallowed and wet her lips.

"Cecily came up to say you wished to see me?"

"Yes."

Mother's curt reply set Felicity's heart racing yet again. If that didn't give away her nervousness, her erratic breathing would.

"Please come and take a seat, Felicity." Father extended an arm toward the other wingback chair next to where he stood. "There is a matter we need to discuss with you."

A matter? Felicity took small steps toward the chair but didn't dawdle. Her parents would see right through her purposeful hesitation, and that might make the situation worse. Once seated, she smoothed her hands on the two pieces of custom-made, matching fabric covering the arms. They helped absorb the dampness of her palms as she awaited the start of this discussion.

She looked back and forth between the two before her. Father darted a quick glance at Mother, who cleared her throat with a dainty cough.

"Felicity, dear, it has come to the attention of your father and me that your charity work has been leading you into areas that possess a certain risk for someone of your position." Mother shifted and leveled a direct look at Felicity. "Specifically, the knowledge that you have recently been working at a factory near the river."

Felicity gasped. How had they found out? She'd been extra careful to cover her tracks and eliminate all evidence of her daytime activities. Everyone knew she spent the time helping Mrs. Gibson, but they didn't know about the factory. Felicity knew she'd dishonored her parents by lying. It was inevitable that she'd be discovered. She just didn't expect that day to come so soon. She started to open her mouth, but a wave of Mother's hand silenced the words on her lips.

"Your father and I have supported you for several years in the many endeavors in which you have been involved. We have permitted you to pay visits to undesirable areas of town with only a driver as your chaperone, and we have looked the other way when reports have come back to us of you taking your work a little too far when it comes to your generosity."

Remorse descended as Mother reminded her of the unwise choices she'd made in the past. Felicity wished those mistakes could remain unmentioned. She might have been naïve enough to fail to recognize the dangerous attention of that father of the one family or to be so taken with the two young boys that one time that she didn't see they were taking advantage of her. But the current work she did was nothing like those experiences. Convincing Mother and Father, though, wouldn't be easy.

"Thankfully, those errors in judgment have been minor,"

Mother continued. "And they haven't caused our family any harm in regard to wagging tongues or social standing. But this"—she waved one of her hands in a wispy motion—"this factory work has caused several matrons among my acquaintances to question our position of authority where you're concerned."

Felicity wanted to speak out on her own behalf and defend her actions. But she knew her place. Mother would allow her rebuttal when the time came. For now she was expected to sit quietly and listen.

"Now as I said, your father and I support your endeavors to assist those less fortunate. But I cannot abide the idea of my daughter interacting with the surly sorts and others of questionable standing who reside by that area of the river. After all, it's not only your safety that concerns us. We also have our reputation at stake."

Reputation. As if this small affair with which she occupied herself would cause any lasting harm to the years her parents—and grandparents before them—had spent establishing themselves among the upper echelon of Detroit.

Father shifted and leaned forward, and Felicity turned to look at him while he spoke.

"What your mother means is that we don't wish to see you doing anything that might bring you harm. Our social standing *is* important." He cast a reproving look in Mother's direction and returned his attention to Felicity. "We know you have a strong desire to help those in need, and your service brings glory and honor to God. But your safety is of prime concern. We cannot guarantee that you won't meet with undesirable circumstances if you insist upon spending time in certain areas without a chaperone or without telling us where you've been."

Father slid his left hand along the back of the chair as

he moved around it to take a seat, angling his body toward Felicity.

"Now why don't you tell us more about this current project of yours? Help us fill in the holes of what we're hearing."

Felicity paused before speaking. She'd worked out an explanation in her mind as her parents talked, but Father's words about honoring God made her rethink her planned speech. Mimicking her mother's posture, she took a deep breath and released it quietly as she sent a prayer heavenward for help. She meant well, and her motives were pure. However, more than a pure heart would be needed here. She'd lied, and she had to face the consequences. Hopefully her parents would understand. This had to work. Otherwise Father might forbid her from continuing. And she didn't want that. She smoothed her clammy hands on the material of her skirt and swallowed past the tightness in her throat.

"Yes, it's true that I have taken a job at the soap and candle factory along the river."

Mother gasped, but Father stayed her verbal outcry with his hand and nodded at Felicity to continue.

"But I assure you I am in no danger in the position where I've been assigned. And I don't intend to remain there long. When Mrs. Gibson delivers her baby and is given permission to end the doctor's orders, she'll seek work again at the factory, and my assistance will no longer be needed in that regard."

She made sure to include Mother but spent more time looking at Father. He would likely be more lenient and understanding. However, she still had to be careful or he'd issue an edict, and it would mean the end to her work.

"My supervisor has placed me alongside two other girls who come from modest families. I have come to enjoy the work I do very much. It's rare to see any altercations or threat to our safety, and a supervisor is in constant motion, circulating throughout the work areas. We also submit regular status reports. If evidence of a problem arises, it's handled immediately."

Father leaned back in his chair. "It does relieve me to hear of such a tightly run operation."

Mother's eyes filled with worry. "But what about the walk through that part of town? It is the business district, if I'm not mistaken."

"Oh, I don't walk alone, Mother. Brandt makes sure that I arrive at the gate safely."

Oh no! Had she just let Brandt's name slip from her tongue? She'd been so careful up to this point. And now this. She'd better make the best of it.

"Brandt?" Mother's voice raised half an octave. "Do you mean to tell us that you are keeping company with a young man who also works in the factories?" Reproach spilled over into every facet of Mother's features and body language. "Felicity Chambers, have we not taught you better than that?"

"But, Mother, Brandt isn't anything like some of those men. We meet along the way and share enjoyable conversation to make the time pass more quickly. His manners are impeccable, and he treats me with a great deal of respect."

Father regarded her through slightly narrowed eyes. "Does this young man have a last name?"

"I believe he said it's Dalton. We only introduced ourselves the one time, but I'm fairly certain I'm recalling it correctly."

Mother leaned forward. "What else do you know about him? Where does he live? Who are his parents? What type of lifestyle does he lead when he's not at work? Why has he singled you out to escort from the obvious dozens of other young ladies who work there?"

"Davinia, please." Father's low voice rumbled as he muttered the soft reprimand. "Let's give our daughter the benefit of the doubt before assuming too much."

Felicity shot him silent thanks for interceding. He might not support Mother's style of interrogation, but he still had questions in his eyes. She knew she'd disappointed them both. But she had been so sure she'd done the right thing. Now, despite Father's apparent patience, he quietly demanded answers. He wasn't satisfied yet.

"We appreciate your honesty, Felicity," Father began. "You could have denied everything and forced us to take other measures. But you didn't. However, without knowing more about this young man you've mentioned, we must caution you against developing a rapport with him."

"But, Father, it isn't like that at all." She unclasped her hands and rested them on the arms of the chair. "He is only a friend. Nothing more." At least that much was true in reality. Her thoughts were another matter. "We met on my first day of work. He was starting his first day at the refinery. It didn't take us long to realize that merging our respective paths wouldn't add any time. And it provides us both with a companion for the walk."

Father pressed his lips into a thin line. "And you say he is always respectful?"

"I have never found a single fault with his manners."

"Hmm." Father inhaled and released his breath in a loud sigh. He was about to make a judgment. She prayed it would be in her favor. "Very well. You have always provided clear explanations in the past, despite initial misgivings. And because of that we will trust you now. But be careful where this young man is concerned. Use wisdom and exercise caution. Otherwise, your mother and I will put a stop to your work." He turned toward Mother. "Davinia? Is that agreeable to you?"

Mother nodded and pursed her lips. "I do not see any cause to end your charity work, Felicity dear. But I agree with your father's word of caution. This young man might be respectful and possess manners that make you trust him, but I do not want to see you develop a relationship beyond friendship with him. There are more than enough young men right here in the Grosse Pointe district who would be happy to receive your affections. Guard your heart, and remember your place."

There it was again. That constant reminder of her social standing and the distinctive line drawn that separated her from everyone else who wasn't like them. Just once she'd like to see people judged according to their character. Not just by their financial holdings.

"Thank you, Mother. Father." She regarded them each in turn and dipped her head in acknowledgment. "I will take what you've said this evening to heart and not forget. It means a great deal to me that you trust me to make the right decisions. And I promise that you have no reason to worry. Should any risk develop, you have my word that I will cease all involvement."

Felicity prayed that day would never come as long as she was helping Mrs. Gibson. Her work and the time spent with Brandt meant more to her than anything else she'd done. Brianna and Laura made up for the daily absence of her childhood friends, and the skills she was learning gave her a feeling of accomplishment. A rather substantial void would exist if she had to give up everything—especially Brandt.

Father stood and extended his right hand toward Mother to help her rise before tucking her hand into the crook of his arm. "Now that we have that settled, let's adjourn to the dining room. I believe Rebecca has supper ready to serve." He looked at Felicity with a twinkle in his eyes. "Your brother has invited his fiancée to join us. They and your sister are no doubt anxiously awaiting our arrival so they can eat."

Felicity stood as her parents stepped past her. Just as she moved to follow, Father reached out and ran the backs of his fingers down her cheek. He gave her a loving smile, and she returned it with one of her own.

As they exited the parlor, Felicity stared at their backs. That conversation had gone better than she'd hoped. It could have been much worse. At least she was allowed to continue her work and her friendship with Brandt. If she wanted things to stay that way, though, she must be careful. And where Brandt was concerned, that became more and more difficult with each passing day.

eight

Brandt plopped down on the grass beside Felicity, and she jumped in response.

"Sorry. I didn't mean to scare you."

She waved him off. "It's all right. I must have been daydreaming."

Her voice trembled a little. She wasn't comfortable. That much was clear. He held a tin cup full of water in one hand and his lunch pail in the other as he assessed the secluded spot. A handful of people walked in the distance. The rear walls of the buildings kept them hidden from view of the streets, and the river to the south afforded a natural barrier. None of Father's employees would find him here. But now he wondered if this meeting was a wise one. She didn't need to see his hesitation, though. Felicity was already nervous.

"See? What did I tell you?" Brandt announced with forced pride. "This is the perfect spot."

Felicity looked around them with a guarded expression. "It is out of the way. That's for certain." She hesitated a moment then nodded. "But it does appear to be a good choice. We can eat our lunches quickly and not worry about anyone from the refinery or factory interrupting or delaying us. We don't have long for our lunch break."

Brandt snapped his fingers and pointed at her. "Exactly."

She took a bite of an apple but still looked to the left and right, as if trying to determine if anyone was watching them. He was the one who had to be concerned about a manager or supervisor spotting him in this non-business-related situation. They would report back to Father for certain. She had nothing to worry about. So why was she so jumpy?

"How did you find this place?"

Brandt jerked his gaze back to hers and stuttered. "Oh, um, I was out walking one day and stumbled upon it. Seemed like it would be a good place for an impromptu picnic." At least that wasn't a lie. She didn't need to know he had found it during one of his routine checks of his father's business holdings.

Felicity shifted her focus and regarded her apple as if it held some special secret. "It does seem lovely."

Her voice was so soft he had to strain to hear her above the lapping of the water against the shoreline and the noise from the nearby factories. It was time for a change of subject.

"How has your morning at work been?"

Felicity looked at him and smiled. "Quite well. And yours?"

He shrugged. "There haven't been any surprises or problems."

"We had a small issue when one of the churns for the soap stopped working. But Laura figured out there were some pieces of wax that had managed to get into the space between the teeth of the crank, causing it to skip and eventually jam."

Finally. A subject she seemed to embrace. At least the only problems they had were cranks breaking and wax melting wrong. The machines at the refinery were far more dangerous. "That didn't set you back by much in productivity, did it?"

"Not much, no." Felicity took a bite of her sandwich and chewed slowly then swallowed. "Laura wasn't too happy with the dirt stains on her clothing, though." She giggled. "She forgot to tie on her apron this morning, so when she had to reach in between the teeth, the dust and grime transferred from the crank to her."

Brandt chuckled at the mental image he formed from her description. The ladies he normally found among his acquaintance would never set foot in a place like the factory, let alone reach their hands inside a piece of machinery to fix a broken crank. The mere idea of dirt usually sent them running off to change clothes.

"Well, at least she fixed the problem. And working at the factory, she likely gets oil and wax on her often."

"Not in the least. I believe she was upset because she's supposed to meet a young gentleman after the final whistle blows. Rumor has it he'll be walking her home." Felicity smiled and took a drink from her tin cup.

Brandt waggled his eyebrows. "Aha. That explains it. She's besotted."

Her lips tightened, preventing the water she'd just drunk from escaping.

He laughed and placed his hands in his lap as he attempted to school his expression into one of nonchalance. It was no use. "I'm sorry," he said through barely contained chuckles. "I do thank you, though, for sparing me the spray of your drink."

With a swallow and dainty clearing of her throat, Felicity once again regained her composure. "You are most welcome," she replied, raising her cup again to her lips. "But I cannot guarantee that should a repeat occurrence take place, you will remain free from harm."

It took Brandt a moment to process what she'd just said. He narrowed his eyes at the playful threat laced between her words. She spoke with such calm, her expression devoid of any mischief. He couldn't tell if she was flirting or serious. And she likely preferred it that way. Such a unique blend of sophistication and affability.

He reached into his pail and retrieved a sandwich wrapped in a red-and-white-checkered cloth. Holding it up for her perusal, he raised his eyebrows and grinned. "Well? What do you think?"

"About your sense of humor or the fact that you finally brought a sandwich for lunch?" She took a final bite of her apple, the corners of her lips turning up slightly as she chewed.

"My—" He paused. Wait a minute. Had she just given him a taste of his own medicine? He clenched his jaw and raised his chin a fraction of an inch. "The sandwich, of course."

She swallowed and tossed the core into her pail. "In that case, I approve. You simply do not know what you're missing eating all those cookies and cakes."

He leaned back on his elbows and regarded her through half-lidded eyes. "Well, I thought it might be wise to give your suggestion a try." Taking a bite of the ham and mustard between the bread, he released an overexaggerated groan. "Mmm. It's the best sandwich I've ever had."

Felicity covered her mouth and giggled. "And probably the first."

Brandt shook a finger in her direction. "That's not true. I seem to recall my mother making some when I was a boy."

She reached for her own sandwich and daintily set about unfolding a checkered cloth that matched his. When she looked up at him again, she grinned. "And since then you've likely taken your fill of whatever was convenient."

He propped himself on one elbow. "I'll have you know our cook prepares delicious meals and makes sure each one of us eats some of everything she's made."

Felicity paused with her sandwich midway to her mouth and stared, her lips parted. "You have a cook?" she managed, her voice thick.

Oh no! How was he going to get out of this one?

"In a manner of speaking. She lives with us and is part of the family. Cooking is how she earns her keep and pays for her room."

She cocked her head and remained silent for several moments. Brandt could feel the heat warm his neck and creep toward his cheeks. If she figured out he had a butler and maidservants as well, there'd be no end to the long line of questions she'd ask.

"I can understand that," she finally said with a nod. "Mrs. Gibson has a girl working in her home to take care of the children and the house. She doesn't live with Mrs. Gibson, but she just as easily could."

Brandt didn't dare offer anything more. He might give away the address of his family's three-story town house or some other critical piece of information that would reveal his charade. Time to get the focus off of him.

"What about you?" He took a small bite of ham and swallowed. "Does this girl working for Mrs. Gibson make your meals, too?"

"Oh no! I don't live with Mrs. Gibson."

He drew his eyebrows together. "But I thought you walked to work from there every morning."

She finished her sandwich and shook out the crumbs from the cloth before putting it back in her pail. Then she dusted off her hands and placed them in her lap. "I do, but I walk there from home before that."

"And where is home?"

"Um, not too many blocks from there."

Now *she* was the one being evasive with a nondescript answer. Perhaps there was something she didn't want to tell him. Or she might be ashamed of where she lived.

"So you found out Mrs. Gibson had to quit, and you offered to share your wages until she recovers?"

"Yes."

"Don't your own folks need your wages, too?"

Felicity yanked the stem of a dandelion weed from the

ground and twirled it between her fingers. "Well, they have my older brother, Zach, to help."

He pushed himself to a sitting position and leaned forward. Softening his voice, he tried to coax out a little more about her home life. Maybe it would give him more insight into her background.

"But I get the feeling they don't exactly approve of this."

A pained expression flitted across her face before she had the chance to hide it. "They would definitely prefer it if my work were not the factory, but they don't mind the temporary help I'm offering."

If only he could take away the hurt she was feeling and replace it with the carefree nonchalance she'd always shown. Then again, if he did that, he might not find out anything more about this young woman who'd become such an important part of his life.

"Have you told them you're not exactly in any danger working where you are?"

"Yes." She inhaled then puffed out her cheeks and blew on the white seeds of the weed. "And I even told them that I had you to walk with me."

Brandt reached out and covered the hand in her lap with his own, offering her a slight grin. "Well, if they care about you, as it seems they do, telling them you're keeping company with me might not reassure them in the way you had hoped."

⁂

Felicity looked down at the hand covering hers, his tanned skin a stark contrast to her pale peach shade. She gave him a wary look. "Mother did mention her concerns about that."

Actually, if truth be told, Mother had overreacted in her interrogation regarding Brandt. Father hadn't been too pleased, either, but at least he had maintained a cool head about it all.

"And what about your father?" Brandt continued, as if he'd

read her thoughts. "I'd think he'd want to keep his daughter safe, too."

"Yes. But he was more willing to trust me when I told him there was no cause for concern." She toyed with the idea of removing her hand from underneath his, but it felt so good to have his touch and reassurance.

"I take it this conversation happened rather recently."

She inhaled a sharp breath. "Why do you say that?"

Brandt leaned back and rested his forearms on his knees. She immediately felt the loss of warmth from his withdrawn hand, but his nearness still offered a great deal of comfort in its place.

"I noticed when I first sat down that you seemed a bit distracted. And you weren't yourself. That easygoing manner of yours was missing."

Felicity ducked her chin. "Oh." And she had hoped her teasing remarks and smiles might cover up the inner turmoil. Obviously they hadn't. Brandt had seen right through her unsuccessful attempts. And now he wanted to know more.

She saw his hand before his fingers touched her chin as he raised her head to meet his gaze. "Hey," he said softly. "You can't be expected to be blithe all the time. Life isn't that perfect."

He moved his index finger back and forth on the underside of her chin. She quelled the shiver that started somewhere near the base of her spine. Instead, she got lost in the coffee-colored depths of his caring eyes.

As if he had read her mind, he jerked his hand back and put some distance between them.

"Sorry about that." He averted his gaze for a brief second then released a short sigh. "So what was the outcome of this conversation?"

Felicity blinked a few times. Conversation? Oh, right. The

one with her parents about her work and Brandt. She'd better get a handle on her emotions. And fast.

"It was good."

A dimple in his right cheek appeared, accompanying his grin. "Just good?"

She shrugged. "Well, as I mentioned, Father was more willing to trust me to make the right decisions. Mother wasn't quite so sure, but she eventually agreed as well." She broke off a few blades of grass and played with them. "Of course, this came with the obligatory reminder that I need to be careful at all times and not let down my guard where anyone is concerned."

"Especially not with strange young men who offer to escort you safely to the factory."

"Yes. That's almost exactly what they said, although it was more inferred than spoken."

He resumed his former position with arms on his knees. "At least they seem understanding."

"For now." Felicity nodded. "But I still have to be careful."

His hand touched hers again. "I promise not to give them any reason to worry more than they already are. And if it helps, I'll even tell them so myself."

She straightened. "Oh no! That won't be necessary."

Gracious. If they were to meet Brandt, there would be no way she'd be permitted to continue her association with him. Her parents would judge him based upon his clothing, no matter how clean he kept himself or how mannerly he was. No, it was best he remain nothing more than a name to them.

"All right. All right." He chuckled and patted her hand. "I'll stay a faceless escort if you wish."

"Thank you."

Oh how she wished he could become something more than that. His concern for her warmed her heart. And the softness in his eyes all but wore down her resolve to keep those parts of her life a secret. No. She dared not risk it. She walked on thin ice as it was.

If she didn't control the circumstances as much as possible, that thin layer would crack and she'd be pulled beneath the safe surface into the turbulent waters below. If the crashing jolt of reality coming face-to-face with the day-to-day world she'd created didn't ruin her, her parents' reactions to the truth would.

The whistles at the factories blew loud and strong, releasing clouds of steam high into the air and signaling the end to their lunch break.

"Looks like it's time to get back to work." Brandt stood and dusted off his pants, then retrieved his cap and slapped it on his head. He held out a hand to assist her. "You ready?"

She placed her hand in his and smiled. "Not exactly, but what other choice do we have?" Standing, she fluffed out the folds of her skirts.

Brandt bent to pick up her pail and grabbed his as well.

"Not a lot. But just think. Only a few more hours and we'll be done for the day. I'm sure the time will fly."

"Yes, and then we have our one day of rest and Sunday services before starting all over again."

He handed her pail to her and mumbled something that sounded like, "Don't remind me."

"What was that?"

Brandt cleared his throat. "Uh, nothing. We do have one day of reprieve, and it's a much-needed one." He started walking, and she had to almost jog to keep up with him. "We'd better get back. Don't want to be late and receive a demerit for tardiness."

Well, the least she could do was show her appreciation for the enjoyable thirty minutes they'd shared.

"Thank you for joining me for lunch. And for finding this little spot."

He stopped and turned toward her. "You're welcome. We should do it again."

"Perhaps."

"Well, off I go." He touched two fingers to the brim of his cap and saluted. "Until next week."

Felicity rushed toward the factory and stepped inside with two minutes to spare. She had such a good time with him today. In fact, every time they were together, he managed to lift her spirits and make her forget her troubles. . .even if only for a little while. But that was where she had to watch out. If she wasn't careful, the sincerity in those deep brown eyes of his would be her undoing. No. Forgetting simply wasn't an option.

nine

"Felicity!" Laura ran toward her from across the courtyard later that day, waving a slip of paper high above her head. She stumbled but caught herself before a fall and continued her advancement.

Felicity paused. What scheme did Laura have in mind now? Felicity had hoped to step out for a breath of fresh air. They only had fifteen minutes. Laura had better make this fast.

The young woman halted in front of Felicity and doubled over, breathing hard. "I'm sorry," she said in a whoosh. "I didn't. . .mean to. . .interrupt. . .your break." Laura took several deep breaths and stood straight. "But this notice was just posted on the bulletin board near the front entrance."

"What does it say?" Felicity tried to catch sight of some of the words, but Laura wouldn't hold the paper still. "If you'd stop waving it, I might be able to read it."

Laura bit her lower lip and offered a sheepish grin. "Oh, sorry." She extended her hand with the note. "Here. Read it for yourself. But be quick about it. I have to put it back when we're done."

Felicity took the paper from Laura and scanned the brief missive. When she finished, she lifted her eyes over the top of the paper, quirked one corner of her mouth, and raised her eyebrows. "You came running all the way across the courtyard for this?"

Laura's shoulders slumped. "What do you mean, 'for this'?" she mimicked. "It's a picnic! In a park by the river!"

"Yes." Felicity nodded. "I read that."

"But aren't you excited?" She spun in circles, her arms straight out to the sides, making her look like one of those seeds from a maple tree twirling to the ground. "Just imagine. They're closing the factories on a Saturday for this. That's big news! And everyone's been invited." She paused and gave Felicity a smug look. "That means the young men from the refinery, too."

"Ah, so now I know why you're anticipating this auspicious event."

Laura tilted her head. "Aus-what event?"

She did it again. Felicity closed her eyes a second then opened them. She had to be more careful about her word choices. But sometimes they just slipped out. "Auspicious. It means fortunate or promising."

Laura straightened with a quick jerk of her head, a wide smile transforming her face. "Oh, then yes. It will be very promising, maybe for you and Brianna, too, if you don't botch it."

"What are we going to botch?"

They both turned to face Brianna, who joined them.

Felicity held out the paper. "Laura here is exclaiming over the great opportunities we'll all have at the upcoming picnic hosted by the management of the factories here along the river."

Brianna snatched it and held it up to read. She gave Felicity an amused look. "Oh, she is? And why do you think there will be 'great opportunities,' Laura?"

Laura stamped her foot and shoved her fists against her hips. "Oh, you two are such spoilsports. It's a wonder you manage to have any fun at all."

"Just because we don't have your type of fun, Laura, doesn't mean we don't have any." Felicity gave her friend a light shove in the shoulder. "Besides, why are you so interested in other men from the refinery? What happened to that young gentleman who was supposed to walk you home the other day?"

Brianna leaned forward and tapped one finger against her lips. "Yes. You never said a thing about him afterward. So let's have it."

The young woman shrugged and dropped her arms as if the meeting she'd anticipated for days meant nothing at all. "He walked me home, we said good night, and that was the end of it."

Brianna crossed her arms and smirked. "Not your type, or are you looking to increase your options a bit more?"

"I'll have you know," Laura replied, turning to bring her face within inches of Brianna's, "that I am in no hurry to marry the first man who crosses my path." She stuck her nose in the air and closed her eyes. "I have standards, thank you."

Brianna gave Laura a little shove and laughed. "You are such an easy target when it comes to men."

"That's because I have them in my life," Laura said, her pointed words succinct.

"And who says I don't?" Brianna replied.

Laura stopped her verbal onslaught with a quick halt. Her entire demeanor changed from puffed-up self-confidence to supreme interest in Brianna's last remark. Felicity stood in silence watching the verbal volley. There was no way she dared interject, or they might turn everything around on her and start the interrogation about Brandt. With her feelings for him so uncertain, questions from her friends were the last thing she needed.

Laura clasped her hands in front of her and stared wide-eyed at Brianna like a little girl in front of the candy jars at the mercantile. "Do you mean you've been keeping company with a young man and you haven't said anything to us?"

Brianna shrugged it off with a nonchalant air. "I didn't say that."

"Then why did you say what you did?"

"To see you react the way you are right now," Brianna replied with a wink and a grin.

Laura huffed. "Well, I never!"

"Like I said. You make an easy target." She reached for Laura's hands and gave them a quick squeeze. "But that's why we love you."

Laura pretended offense at the good-natured teasing, but she relaxed her shoulders and cast a quick glance from the corner of her eye at Brianna. Everything was fine again. The two were still best friends.

"So what about this picnic?"

Leave it to Laura to get the conversation back on track to where she wanted to steer it.

Felicity took the paper back from Brianna and read it again. "I believe it sounds like a truly splendid idea. It will be a delight to escape the cavernous surroundings of the factory and bask in the warm sunshine for a change."

When no response came from either of the two girls, Felicity looked up. They stood staring, their mouths hanging slightly open.

"What? Did I say something wrong?"

"Truly splendid?" Laura echoed.

"Cavernous surroundings?" Brianna added.

"Honestly." Laura expelled a sigh and brushed her bangs out of her face. "If we didn't know better, we might mistake you for one of those hoity-toity gems from the Pointe."

If only they knew. Felicity chuckled, the hollow sound and her pounding heart making her palms sweat. She brushed them against her skirt but made it look like she was removing pieces of dirt instead.

"I'm sorry. I guess it's all the books I read. Sometimes those words just spill out." Felicity hunched her shoulders and splayed her hands, palms up. "If it happens again, just smack my arm and let me know."

"Oh, you can count on that!" Brianna said with a twinkle in her eye.

"Perfect." Laura draped her arms around the shoulders of Felicity and Brianna and steered them toward the west entrance. "Now can we get back to talking about our plans for the picnic?"

⁂

One week later Felicity stood at the edge of the park and stared. What a sight to behold! There had to be hundreds of people gathered on the grassy areas, and that didn't include the number in small dinghies or rowboats on the water, or even those brave enough to risk the frigid river. It might be August, but she'd stepped in that river on the hottest day of the year. And nothing would make her repeat that experience.

"Well, don't just stand there! Come on!" Laura turned her face to the wind and sniffed. "I can smell popcorn and fried chicken. And the music is so lively. Let's go!" She ran ahead of them, almost bouncing along the way.

Brianna turned toward Felicity. "Some days I wonder if she'll ever be less excitable."

"If she did that, she wouldn't be Laura," Felicity countered with a grin.

Brianna sighed. "True."

Felicity tucked the handles of their picnic basket with a few extra treats into the crook of her right elbow and grabbed Brianna's arm with her left as they followed in Laura's wake. "You have to admit, though, there is never a dull moment with her."

Brianna tilted back her head and laughed. "No. You're right about that. Still, I wonder what it will take for her to settle down."

"Are you saying you envy her exuberance?"

"Me?" Brianna slapped her free hand against her chest, her top lip curling a little. "No, but I look forward to when we meet the man who will tame her."

A giggle escaped Felicity's lips at the thought of a man being able to tame Laura's wild ways. "Now *that* would be a sight to see."

"All right. Let's find a good place to set out our blanket and food. Then we can go see who else is here."

Felicity spied an area a little off to the side and out of the way. Perfect. Just the right amount of shade and seclusion, but still at the edge of those gathered on the ground nearby. Brianna was looking in the opposite direction, but Felicity gave her a tug.

"Why do you want to go way over here?" Brianna jerked her thumb over their shoulders toward the men onstage performing a spirited number with their instruments. "The center of activity is over there."

Exactly where she didn't want to be. What if someone who knew her recognized her? She would never be able to explain her presence or her acquaintance with them to Brianna and Laura. And what about Brandt? He was sure to be here. It was only a matter of time until he spotted her, too. She hoped to be alone when that happened, and she wouldn't be if they were in the middle of the crowd.

"I know, but I thought it might be better to have a little peace and quiet." She stepped into the clear space and set down the basket, lifting the lid to retrieve the cloth on which they'd sit.

Brianna grabbed one end and stepped away to help Felicity spread out the cloth. "All right. We'll probably want the quiet after being here a few hours."

Thankfully they were in a part of town that her friends

didn't frequent. But that didn't mean she was safe. She couldn't let down her guard even for a minute.

"I'm going to find Laura and see what kind of trouble she's gotten herself into." Brianna walked around Felicity then turned to look over her shoulder. "You going to be all right here?" She grinned. "I'm sure it won't be long before Laura finds us again."

Felicity waved her away. "I'll be fine. Don't worry about me. Go and take a look at everything. There will be plenty of time for me to do the same later."

"Bye."

She watched as Brianna disappeared into the crowd. Truth be told, sitting alone was exactly what she preferred. The less she wandered around, the less chance of being discovered. How would she ever explain her clothing and association with girls like Brianna and Laura if someone from the Pointe district were to appear? It might not be likely in this area, but anything was possible. Of course, if Brandt were with her, perhaps they might think she was someone else and keep on walking.

"Excuse me, but is anyone sitting here?"

Brandt!

Felicity raised a hand to shade her eyes and stared up at the shadowed figure standing before her. It was as though her thoughts had conjured him into appearing.

"No." She lowered her head and extended her hand toward the space in front of her. "Please. Sit down."

"Don't mind if I do," he said, snapping his suspenders against his chest.

As soon as he was settled, he swiped off his cap and dropped it beside him. Shocks of unruly hair shot out in all directions. It reminded her of when they first met. Felicity giggled. He couldn't be more endearing.

"What?" He raised his hands to his head and offered a rueful smile. "All right, so I forgot to brush my hair this morning." Grabbing his cap in his fist, he held it out in front of him. "That's why I have this," he said and let the cap fall once more.

Felicity covered her mouth and spoke through her fingers. "If you don't mind, I don't mind."

Brandt slapped his hands together as if ridding them of dirt or crumbs, then plunked them down on his crossed legs. "Good. Now that we have that settled." He rose up just a bit on his knees and sniffed in the general direction of the picnic basket. "What are we having for dessert?"

Felicity tugged the basket a little closer to her. Her friends would tar and feather her if she gave up any of their sweets. "That is for Brianna and Laura."

He chuckled and splayed his hands in defense. "I was only teasing." Patting his stomach, he sighed, the sound full of contentment. "Besides, I already had my fill from a few of the vendors on the other side of the park. The barbecued beef was delicious. Decided to take a walk and ended up finding you."

She smoothed out the folds of her dress and placed her hands in her lap. "We arrived not long ago. Laura ran off as soon as she smelled the food and heard the music, so Brianna went to find her."

"And left you alone?"

Felicity pointed to the basket. "Someone had to stay and look out for our belongings."

"Good point."

❧

Brandt leaned back on his elbows and regarded Felicity for a moment. He'd seen the trio the moment they arrived, but he waited for the opportune moment to approach. At least he didn't have to wait long. And since he'd already eaten, he had no reason not to spend the rest of the time with Felicity. Or at least as long as she would allow.

The place she'd chosen was perfect. He'd already dodged one of the supervisors once. He didn't want to do it again. Some of them knew of his "assignment" from Father, but his friends from the refinery didn't. And they'd invited him. It was best to save face and not risk anything more. Why she preferred to be away from the center of activity, though, he didn't know.

"So," he said by way of continuing the conversation. "Is there anything you wish to see here at the park today? You've already mentioned the music. But would you like to see some of the entertainment on the other side?"

She pursed her lips and tilted her head, the long braid she'd fashioned falling over her shoulder. A few wisps framed her face, giving her a cute and appealing image.

"Well, I heard they were going to have mimes performing. That might be interesting to see."

He nodded. "The mimes are here, and in the part I saw, they reminded me of the statue near city hall."

"Do you mean the soldiers' monument?"

"You know about it?" Now that was a bit of a surprise. It didn't seem like the type of thing that would interest her or be anywhere near where she spent most of her time.

"Yes. My parents told me about it when they first unveiled it three years ago. Generals Sheridan, Custer, and Burnside were present for the ceremony, they said. And I've seen a drawing of it as well."

"It's definitely something worth seeing. The octagonal shapes, the eagles on pedestals, the four men standing in place of the Navy, Infantry, Cavalry, and Artillery branches of the U.S. Army. Even the plaques dedicated to the four Union leaders are impressive."

"Don't forget the Indian warrior, Michigan, standing at the top," Felicity pointed out.

"With a sword in her right hand and a shield in her left. How could I miss her?"

"All constructed in bas-relief style, I believe," she added, casting a surreptitious glance to her left.

"That's right." How had she known something like that? That wouldn't be a fact she'd be able to infer from a drawing. He shrugged it off. "And it couldn't be in a better place. Right at the center of five principal streets and at the tip of Campus Martius Park."

"And how do you know so much about it?"

He wondered how long it would take her to ask him that. "I get around," Brandt replied, attempting to keep his tone nonchalant. He contemplated not sharing so much, but he didn't know what else to say. Besides, architecture in the city was a fairly safe topic. "Perhaps I can show it to you sometime."

She hesitated, her eyes flashing with a mixture of sadness and delight. What an odd combination.

"That would be nice," she finally said, her voice lacking the enthusiasm of just a moment ago. Her eyes again looked to the left and right.

Was it something he'd said? Did she want to be with someone else or make sure no one saw them together? No. That didn't seem like her at all. Sometimes having conversations with her had him feeling like he was on the losing end of a guessing game. At any given moment, she could act like two different people instead of the same young woman. Confusion like this could drive a guy crazy.

The song floating from the stage reached their ears, and Felicity tilted her head. Her face didn't register recognition, and a second later, she turned back to him.

"Who is that playing?"

Brandt looked at the two men onstage. "The younger one is Clayton Grinnell. He's attending the university and has a keen interest in pianos. The other older gentleman is Frederick Stearns."

She gasped. "The pharmacist?"

"You recognize his name?"

"Father was sent to his offices once for some special medicine to help his brother with a heart condition. He's on East Jefferson near the MacArthur Bridge, right?"

"Right."

There was no end to the surprises Felicity had hiding up her sleeve. She should pursue a career as a magician with the way she succeeded at throwing him off track. Just when he thought he had her figured out, she threw another twist into his obvious misconceptions.

"Mr. Stearns is a savvy businessman, and I've heard he loves collecting instruments. I'm not surprised to see him here with some of the men and their pieces that have probably been in their families for years."

A well-dressed couple strolled nearby, and Felicity stiffened with a soft gasp. She turned her head in the opposite direction and found the grass next to the cloth on which they sat to be quite fascinating. The pair hesitated a moment and looked at her but continued on their way.

"Is something wrong, Fe. . .Miss Chambers?" In his mind, he called her by her given name, but it wasn't right to do so out loud.

She peered from the corner of her eye at the path where the couple had been, then slowly resumed her previous position. Her behavior today seemed a bit odder than usual.

"I wanted to keep an eye out for Laura and Brianna. They are likely to return at any moment." She stopped then brightened as if she'd found the perfect explanation. "If they see you here with me, they'll pester you with a never-ending stream of questions."

"Are you saying you'd like me to leave?"

"No!" she answered a little too quickly. "That is. . .I. . .uh. . . I don't want you to be forced to endure their interrogation."

A tinge of pink stained her cheeks, and she ducked her head. Despite her erratic and somewhat befuddling behavior, Brandt couldn't be upset. She was right, though. She'd come with her friends today, and he didn't have the right to command much more of her time.

"Actually, my friends are no doubt wondering where I am, too." He placed his fists on the ground and shoved upward as he stood. "I hope you'll get over and see the mimes. And make sure you sample some of the popcorn from the vendor cart."

Her head bobbed, and she again shielded her eyes as she gazed up at him. He wanted nothing more than to stay by her side, but this was not the time or the place. Extending his hand down toward her, he waited until she placed her delicate fingers against his. He bent at the waist and raised her fingers to his lips, placing a brief kiss on her knuckles.

"Until next time."

The smile she bestowed upon him made all the questions about her behavior today inconsequential. He snatched his cap from the checkered cloth, slapped it on his head, and waved a farewell to Felicity. Seeing her away from the factory again had been quite a treat. Other than her frequent glances around the park, she seemed genuinely intrigued by the facts he shared and the points of interests he described. If he had any say at all, there would definitely be a next time.

ten

Brandt stepped back as Bartholomew Sanderson stepped into the hallway from his office and pulled the door shut behind him.

"Where are we headed today?" Brandt asked as he walked beside the manager down the hall and toward the stairs. It wasn't easy continuing this back-and-forth work between management and the main refinery. Some of his friends had begun questioning his sporadic absences. He'd be glad when he could finally make the switch and put all of this behind him. Just one more week.

Sanderson tugged on the sleeves of his chambray shirt and adjusted the string tie at his neck. It must be an important meeting for him to take such care with his appearance.

"The owner of a new bell-casting shop recently moved to Detroit and is interested in the copper we produce." He walked with a purpose, his carriage tall and erect. "Your father tells me it could mean a great deal of money invested in our refinery and his company should this gentleman like what we have to say."

"I recall Father mentioning a man who had been hired to cast some new bells for some of the churches here in the city as well as near city hall." He preceded Sanderson down the stairs and cocked his head over his left shoulder. "Is this the same man?"

"One and the same. That is, the caster isn't the same man as the one we're going to meet," he corrected, his words beating a staccato rhythm matching his descent on the steps.

"This man is the owner of the casting facility."

Brandt pressed down the latch and pushed open the heavy door, holding it for Sanderson, who exited a moment later. "And he makes all the decisions about where to get his supplies."

Sanderson nodded. "Exactly."

"Well, there aren't exactly too many options here in Detroit. If he doesn't agree to partner with us for his needs, he'll have to import them from Canada or even as far away as the Locks up north."

Somehow Brandt had a hard time believing this owner would even consider the expense such a decision would incur. They produced the purest copper and copper elements within a one-hundred-mile radius. The man would be a fool not to invest with them.

"From what I've heard, he's been quite diligent in his research and investigation of the available refineries in the area. This meeting is likely nothing more than a formality, and your father asked me to bring you along for the experience."

Ah, now the truth came out. This might be a bona fide business appointment, but he was only included to learn more about this end of his father's dealings. Brandt didn't mind, though. Felicity had told him earlier in the week that the factory had hired some new workers and the shifts had changed. So she was working fewer hours as the supervisors planned out a new schedule. He would have much preferred sharing lunch with her again, but since she wasn't working today, gaining more understanding of the job he'd soon assume suited him just fine.

"I should have known Father would have arranged something like this."

Sanderson paused at the edge of the refinery gate. "Are you saying you'd rather be back in front of those intolerably hot furnaces and getting covered in soot or burned by the sparks and liquid ore?"

"When you put it that way, I suppose this is the better of the two options." He chuckled and stepped into the street on their way to the nearest trolley line. "But I wish Father would include me in these decisions rather than assuming I'll take part and leaving you to issue the orders."

A rueful expression crossed Sanderson's face. "You do have a point. I'll be sure to bring that up the next time your father comes to meet with me."

"No, no." Brandt brushed off that idea. The last thing he needed was Father thinking he couldn't stand up for himself. "It's only for one more week. I'll speak with him about it tonight. He's always been open to my suggestions in the past. I don't see why this should be any different."

"Yes," Sanderson replied, drawing out the word. "As I recall, you spoke with him not too long ago regarding my overbearing presence in the main areas of the refinery."

Brandt cringed and offered Sanderson an apologetic grin. He probably should have spoken directly to Sanderson, but either way, he knew he was right.

"I did, but only because the other men down there mentioned it more than once. We need to maximize our productivity. Those men felt like they had to keep looking over their shoulders. And when they do that, they're not working."

Sanderson leaned against the lamppost near the corner and crossed his arms. "I didn't say I had a problem with the assessment. I only said that to show you that your father does value your input."

The tinny chime of the trolley's bells sounded, and the horse-drawn cart appeared around the corner. Sanderson shoved off the post and stepped to the curb. Brandt stood beside him.

"All the more reason why I should be the one to speak to him about further instruction where my apprenticeship is concerned."

"Very well." Sanderson shrugged. "If that's the way you wish it to be, I won't stand in the way."

"Thanks. I appreciate that."

The trolley stopped in front of them. The manager climbed aboard, and Brandt grabbed hold of the pole to swing onto the platform. Sanderson shook his head at Brandt's antics. At least he hadn't run behind the cart and hopped onto the rear perch, one hand on the side and the other waving in the wind. He'd been known to do that on more than one occasion.

They rode in silence, and Brandt shifted his thoughts to the conversation he'd have that evening. Father said he was progressing quite well. It wouldn't be long before he could move from apprentice to supervisor. But that meant no more working on the refinery floor. He would soon be overseeing a part of the refinery. The workers under him might not take kindly to the fact that he had worked among them all these months, so perhaps he'd be placed in charge of the initial refining process as the copper was delivered to the plant from the mines.

Once that happened, Felicity was bound to find out. He couldn't exactly avoid the factory. His father had established a solid rapport with the other factory managers along the river. Eventually Brandt would end up meeting with the manager at the factory where Felicity worked. And then how would she react?

Of course, by then Mrs. Gibson could have her baby, and Felicity might surrender her work to leave a possible spot open for Mrs. Gibson. That thought didn't exactly bring a smile to his face. But what if she *was* still there? It could ruin their entire relationship. And he didn't want that to happen. He'd better rethink all this. Maybe he should try to delay his switch to management for just a little longer. At least until he could come up with a viable plan of action.

❧

"That went remarkably well, I must say."

Sanderson almost hopped down the marble stairs in front of Mr. Willoughby's home, his steps light and confident. The bell-casting owner had been quite accommodating. In fact, he'd almost been ready to sign at the X the moment his butler had ushered Brandt and Sanderson into the library.

Brandt dashed down the steps behind Sanderson and grabbed hold of the large knob on top of the rail, swinging himself around to step in line with his manager.

"I agree."

Sanderson cast a glance in Brandt's direction and raised his eyebrows. All right, so he still had a bit of boyishness in him. What difference did that make? He'd rather have a little fun in life than restrict himself to being ostentatious and pompous all the time, like some of the men among Father's acquaintances.

"So where to now?" Brandt asked.

Sanderson tucked one hand in the pocket of his pants and pointed at Brandt with his index finger. "You are free to do as you please. I'm returning to the refinery to finish some ledger work, but your father told me to dismiss you as soon as this errand was complete."

"Really?"

If only Felicity were at the factory this afternoon. He could drop by and catch her as she left. Wouldn't she be surprised by that! That wouldn't happen today, though. And since he didn't even know where she lived, he'd have to wait until next week to see her again.

He glanced ahead of them across the street and almost stopped dead in his tracks.

Felicity?

Brandt blinked several times, shaking his head at what he saw. He had been thinking about her, and now his mind had conjured her where she wasn't. Three young women walked side by side in front of the town houses over there. The one in the middle could be Felicity's twin. His eyes must be playing tricks on him. Those three came from the direction of the elite shops nearby. Felicity would never be keeping company with prim and proper ladies like the two on each side of her. And she'd never be in this part of the city.

But it wasn't her. He had to get that clear in his mind. The resemblance was uncanny. He definitely had to do something about this. He couldn't keep going day in and day out wanting to see her so badly that he saw her when she wasn't there. That could lead to all sorts of problems, none of which he wanted to even acknowledge, let alone claim.

One of the other girls said something, and the young woman in the middle looked over at him. He could have sworn a flash of panic appeared on her face. But from this distance, he couldn't know for sure. Besides, why would she react that way? He didn't know any of those girls. They'd have no reason to give him anything other than a passing glance before continuing on their way.

"Mr. Lawson?"

The deep voice shook him out of his contemplative state. He turned his attention back to the sidewalk in front of him. Bart Sanderson. The refinery. A meeting with Father tonight. That was where his head should be. Not on some apparition his mind had conjured.

"You haven't heard a word I've said, have you?"

"What?" He shook his head and turned toward Sanderson. "I'm sorry, Bart. Guess I got lost in thought."

"That's putting it mildly," Sanderson said with a derisive

snort. "Your mind drifted the moment those three ladies came into view." He smirked. "You know them?"

"No." Brandt sighed. "One of them reminded me of another young lady I know, but it couldn't be her."

"By the way your entire focus shifted, I'd say this young lady's someone special?"

"I guess you could say that."

Sanderson stopped walking. Brandt took a few steps past him before he realized it, so he turned around.

"Look, son, either she is or she isn't. You have to make up your mind. My Marabelle wouldn't have given me a second thought had I not been determined to win her affections." The manager shoved a finger into Brandt's chest. "You don't trifle with women's feelings, my boy. That'll just get you into a load of trouble."

Brandt pushed Sanderson's hand back to the man's side. "Duly noted, sir."

Seemingly satisfied with Brandt's response, Sanderson continued walking. Brandt might as well accompany him until the time came for them to part ways. No sense taking a different route when the direct way was the most efficient.

If only Sanderson's advice concerning Felicity could be followed that easily.

≈

"I do believe I succumbed to the pressure of the clerk and purchased far too many foibles for even *my* tastes." Angela held up the satchels for Felicity and Rachel to see. "How will I ever explain this to Mother?"

"You can't say that we didn't warn you," Rachel pointed out. "Felicity and I both advised you to consider your purchases carefully. I'd say you got what you deserve, spending so recklessly."

"You're just saying that because you weren't able to purchase the items you truly wanted."

"No," Rachel countered, "I'm saying that because I *refrained* from purchasing what I wanted. I intend to return again at a later date to peruse the selections more carefully."

"Sometimes you must simply throw caution to the wind and splurge."

"And sometimes ostentatious expenditures are nothing more than frivolous displays of your wealth."

Felicity glanced over her shoulder again. Her two friends could bicker back and forth the entire length of Beaumont. She had a more pressing matter at hand.

The young man she'd spotted now walked away from her in the opposite direction. He had looked so much like Brandt that she'd stopped to take a second look and almost got tangled in her petticoats. From the way he'd stared for that brief moment, she thought she'd seen recognition in his eyes. But how could that be possible? Brandt wouldn't be walking with Mr. Sanderson. Especially not during the middle of the afternoon. And definitely not in the Pointe district. At least, that's who she thought the man was. No, if he had to meet with Mr. Sanderson, it would be back at the refinery. Even then, the meeting likely wouldn't be a favorable one.

She'd encountered the refinery manager her first day on the job. After signing the work agreement, she'd left Mr. Marshall's office and was almost run over by the man she now knew as Mr. Sanderson. Mr. Marshall greeted him, and even from down below, she had known their conversation was not a pleasant one. The two men exchanged a few heated words, with Mr. Marshall waving his fists in the air. She respected Mr. Marshall a great deal. So the problem must have been with Mr. Sanderson.

"Felicity? Are you all right?"

A hand on her arm made her stop walking. "What?" She

turned to see Rachel looking at her with concern reflected in her eyes.

"I asked if you were all right. Angela and I have been telling you about the cotillion you missed last weekend. But you looked like you were miles away."

Just look at what daydreaming of Brandt did. Conjuring him into existence in place of another young man didn't make him appear for real. She had to stop this.

"I'm sorry, Rachel. Angela." She dropped her shoulders and sighed. "I thought I recognized someone I knew, but he turned out not to be the man I believed him to be."

Angela placed her hands on her hips. "Are you speaking metaphorically or in actuality?"

Felicity giggled. She truly needed this. Straightforward, no-nonsense talk to help her clear her head.

"In actuality."

Rachel maneuvered partway in front of her and Angela, giving Felicity a suspicious look. "Is this the same man you mentioned just before summer? The one who has turned your head in his favor?"

"Yes," she admitted in a whisper. What else could she say? Rachel would see through any lie she told, and Angela would devise a plan to get the information out of her one way or another. She might as well be honest. Well, as honest as possible, anyway.

"Ooh!" Angela clapped her hands and bounced up and down as much as her kid boots would allow. "I knew it. Our dear Felicity has a beau, and she's been holding out on us all this time."

"I never said he was a beau, Angela."

Brandt might be the closest thing she had to a beau, but as of right now their relationship was nothing more than friendship.

"No, you didn't." Angela nodded. "But you didn't say he

wasn't, either," she added with a smirk. "And that grants us the freedom to pursue this line of questioning much further."

Felicity leveled a glare at Angela, but the girl wouldn't be dissuaded.

"Come now, Angela." Rachel placed herself between Felicity and Angela. "Let's not take things too far."

Ah, good. A voice of reason. At least she had Rachel on her side.

"After all," Rachel continued, turning back toward Felicity with a gleam in her eyes. Angela seemed to pick up on it, too, as her entire demeanor changed from a busybody seeking a little gossip to a sleuth on a mission.

Felicity eyed them both. This couldn't be good.

"If we're not careful, we might cause our dear Felicity to become exasperated and despondent. And then we'd never find out the secret to this mysterious gentleman for whom she's been pining away while our backs have been turned."

All right. Enough of this dancing around. Felicity stamped first her right foot then her left, clenching her fists at her sides.

"Now that is not the way it is at all, you two. You're turning this minor little incident into something of extraordinary proportions."

"But of course!" Angela spread her arms wide. "It's what we do best! How else would we successfully manage to extract the necessary information from you if not by extreme measures?"

Felicity looked back and forth at the faces of her two friends. They couldn't be serious. But their faces seemed to indicate their genuine earnestness. Then the corner of Angela's mouth twitched, and she had them.

"Aha!" She wiggled a hand in both of their faces, mirth bubbling up from inside. "I knew it. You two couldn't fool anyone with that ruse."

Rachel placed one hand on her chest and faked an innocent expression. "Why, whatever do you mean?" The batting of her eyelashes only made it worse.

Felicity pressed her lips tight to hold back the laughter, and it came out more like a loud snort before bursting forth from her mouth. That was all it took.

The three of them bent over at the waist, leaning toward one another as giggles and merriment overtook them. A handful of passersby made their way to the other side of the street, their upturned noses and expressions only making the girls laugh that much harder.

Rachel recovered first, straightening and taking several deep breaths to regain her composure. Angela stood as well, her arms holding her middle as she gasped for air. Felicity struggled to catch her own breath. Her sides hadn't hurt that much in months.

"All right. All right." Rachel splayed her hands, palms down, as if attempting to quiet a rowdy group of children. "Let's take our little party to a less conspicuous location, shall we?"

Leave it to Rachel to get everything back under control. Always the voice of reason. She led the three of them to the nearest bench in front of one of the town houses that lined Beaumont. When they all settled in place—Angela with her packages and purchases in her lap and at her feet—Rachel inhaled then released a single breath.

"Now, Felicity. . .dear," she stated, placing emphasis on the last word as she folded her hands in her lap. "Why don't you finish telling us about this gentleman before our efforts to find out more are waylaid yet again."

No way could Felicity escape this one. She just had to make sure not to give away too much in her response. She tucked her legs beneath the bench and adjusted her skirts around her ankles. Looking straight ahead, she delivered the answer she hoped they wanted to hear.

"It's really not as significant as the two of you make it sound." At Angela's expulsion of breath, Felicity rushed to continue. "Yes, there is a gentleman with whom I've been keeping company of late. He is not my beau," she said with a brief pointed look at Angela, who ducked her head. "But he is a good friend."

"And does he have a name?" Rachel asked. "Or shall we create one from our imaginations?"

"He has a name." Felicity placed her palms on her thighs and slid them toward her knees. "But I don't wish to reveal it to you, lest it provide you with enough information to seek him out on your own."

Rachel gasped. "We would never do that!"

"Oh, I would!" Angela piped up. "Anything to get to the bottom of this intriguing mystery."

Felicity raised then lowered her shoulders. "Well, I do so hate to disappoint you both, but there truly isn't much more to say." Actually, there was, but she didn't intend to tell them now. That time would come. Just not today.

"When are you going to see him again?"

"One day next week, I believe." At least she hoped she'd see him. She was going to notify Mr. Marshall on Monday that this would be her final week. Her family had their annual visit to Mackinac Island to attend, and her factory work interfered with that. Her parents would not allow her to stay behind. "I don't know for certain."

And she didn't. There had been days when he didn't meet her at the corner. It didn't happen often, and he tried to let her know ahead of time. But each day didn't guarantee she'd see him. She'd still make sure Mrs. Gibson had enough to provide for her family until the baby was born and Lucy could return to work. Felicity just hoped she'd have a chance to see Brandt before her final day at the factory.

"Very well." Rachel rose and dusted off her skirts. "Since it appears that you don't wish to share the intimate details of your personal affairs, there's nothing left for us to do but return home."

Angela made her way to the sidewalk to stand beside Rachel. "Yes." She jutted her chin into the air an inch or two. "I'm sure we'll find out eventually. And when we do. . ." A devilish gleam entered her eyes, and she rubbed her hands together like the mischievous soul Felicity knew her to be.

Felicity grabbed hold of the railing and pulled herself up to join her friends. They didn't seem hurt or offended, but she had to be sure. Draping her arms around both of their waists, she turned them toward home.

"When that time comes, ladies, I promise you'll be the first to know."

In the meantime, Felicity had some thinking to do.

eleven

"Must you dawdle so, Felicity?" Mother entered Felicity's dressing room, tugging on a pair of white traveling gloves. "The train for Cheboygan departs in less than an hour." She picked up Felicity's valise and placed it on the padded stool. "Your father will not be pleased if we're tardy."

"Yes, Mother. I know." Felicity forced the impatience out of her voice. How many times would Mother remind her of the ticking seconds? She picked up the powder puff from her dressing table and stared at it. As hard as she tried, she couldn't muster up the excitement she once had for this forthcoming journey.

"Felicity." Mother's voice held that tone. The one that meant the next course of action would be calling upon Father to motivate Felicity into action.

"Mother, I know we go to Mackinac Island every summer. But must I go this year?" She'd better have a plausible alternative if she wanted to persuade Mother to agree. "I could stay behind and work with Rebecca on my cooking and general household mistress duties."

"No." Mother pushed the fabric of her gloves into place between her fingers. "You have been rather distracted lately. I do not attempt to know the cause of this despondency, but your father and I have made special plans and we've worked too hard for it all to be spoiled now."

"Plans? What plans?" What did Mother and Father have up their sleeves now?

Mother paid special attention to the wide array of gowns

and outfits that hung in front of the opposite wall. "Oh, nothing too important. We merely contacted a few friends of ours who will also be joining us on the island."

Felicity knew that maneuver all too well. Mother was being evasive. And that could only mean trouble.

"Friends? Why can we not have this little reunion here in Detroit? Why must it be on Mackinac?"

Spurts of air passed between Mother's lips before she gritted her teeth and sucked in a quick breath. "There is no need to mind the reasons. They're of no concern to you. Just know that you *will* accompany your father, your brother and his fiancée, your sister, and me to the island as always. And you will do so with the proper attitude."

Felicity opened her mouth to protest, but Mother waved her off.

"Not another word, Felicity. This discussion is concluded." She brushed past the curtain and stepped into the adjoining bedroom before turning around again. "Finish powdering your face and dressing for travel. I expect to see you downstairs in ten minutes. No more. Is that clear?"

"Yes, Mother," Felicity mumbled.

"What did you say? I'm not sure I heard you correctly."

"Yes, Mother," Felicity repeated, accentuating the two words in crisp tones.

"Very well." Mother disappeared beyond view, but her voice carried through the room. "I shall have Martin fetch your valises. Make certain you have them ready when he arrives."

And with that Mother departed. Felicity slumped against the golden brass bars on the back of her padded chair. She propped her elbow on the dressing table and looked at her reflection. Just once she'd like to feel as if she had complete control over her own life. And she did when she had worked at the factory or devoted herself to her charity work. If only she could spend all her time on charitable services and not on fulfilling the expectations of her mother and every other societal edict that had been placed on her head.

Wait a minute. What was she saying? As much as her charity work fulfilled her, the comforts of the lifestyle afforded her through her parents would not be easy to toss aside. She'd seen the way some of the others without fortune lived. It felt good to be able to select the material she wanted most for a new gown or walk into a shop and purchase what she'd like because she could afford it.

On the other hand, every time she visited Mrs. Gibson or shared meals and conversations with Brianna and Laura, a pang of guilt struck deep inside. And Brandt. He seemed so carefree, despite his existence in a lower class.

Felicity straightened, her arm resting on the edge of the table. If she didn't have her status, though, she wouldn't be able to help people like Mrs. Gibson. So where did she strike the balance?

She sighed. There didn't seem to be an easy answer. And right now she didn't have the time to figure it out. Martin would be here any moment. Mother expected her downstairs in three minutes. And she'd be there. She grabbed her powder puff again and closed her eyes as she blotted it all over her face. Waving the cloud away from her face, she dropped the puff container into her personal valise and stood. With one last glance in the looking glass, she gathered the rope handles of the bag and stepped into her bedroom.

A knock came a moment later. Felicity looked up to see the door push open and Martin peer around the edge.

"Come in, Martin." Felicity pointed to the collection of luggage. "The items are all stacked there against the wall."

"Very good, Miss Felicity." The butler gathered the four pieces under his arms and moved toward the door. "Your sister is already waiting by the front door, and your brother is outside by the carriage. Your mother will likely be in the entryway momentarily."

"As will I, Martin. Thank you."

Felicity snatched her gloves from the small table by the door and slipped them on her hands. At least she had some time of refreshment in the cooler climates of northern Lake Huron. Maybe the fresh air would clear her mind. Getting away for two weeks and a change of scenery just might be the perfect solution to her dilemma.

❧

The steam-powered large lake excursion boat bounced through the choppy water. Felicity grabbed tight to the handrail at the bow as she made her way around to the port side. The train ride on the Michigan Central had lasted overnight as they traveled north, and the summer temperatures had dropped considerably. Out on the lake with the wind blowing in her face, it felt like spring again. They could have taken the train farther north to Mackinaw City, but Father had persuaded the engineer to let them off before that stop to catch a private carriage he'd hired to take them east. This leisurely scenic route suited her just fine. It might take longer than the direct route to the island, but Mother and Father took their family this way every summer, and she wouldn't change a thing.

Setting out from Cheboygan, they traveled by boat across the lake to the east past Pointe Aux Pins and around the southeast side of Bois Blanc Island. Once past the confines of land on the left and right, the lake opened up wide, water in every direction. Other excursion vessels and smaller boats sailed with the heavy winds or fought against them on their way back to shore.

"Oh, Felicity, isn't it just beautiful?" Her younger sister shoved against her then lost her footing as the boat pitched.

She stretched both arms out in front of her and gripped the handrail to right herself again.

Felicity looked out over the expanse of blue water. She inhaled a deep breath of fresh lake air. The stress and strain of the past few weeks ebbed away, leaving nothing but peace in its place. Yes, this time away would be perfect.

"Yes, Cecily, it's breathtaking!"

If only Brandt could see it all. He'd no doubt thrill at the chance to come to a place like this. He seemed to enjoy God's wondrous nature, and this little piece of heaven would enchant anyone. Oh, how she wished she could bring him here.

"I simply cannot wait until we get to Mackinac. We'll get to dance, play, run, and have a grand time."

"Honestly, Cecily, sometimes you can act like such a child." This came from their older brother, Zach, who sidled up on the other side of Felicity, propping his forearms on the port bow.

Cecily scrunched up her nose and made a face at their brother. "That's because I *am* a child, silly."

It looked like thoughts of Brandt would have to wait.

"That's enough, you two." Felicity held up her hands between them. Sometimes she felt more like a mediator than a sister. Being in the middle could be quite a challenge. "And, Cecily," she said with a pointed glance, "you're *not* a child. You're almost fifteen. That's a young woman where you're concerned."

"That's right," Zach chimed in. "Which means you should start acting your age."

Felicity whipped her head in the other direction. "And what about you, Zach? You're older than both of us. Shouldn't *you* be ceasing with this childish behavior as well?"

An unladylike snort came from Cecily, and Felicity's mouth twitched. Zach gave them both a sideways glare then turned his attention back to the lake. At his silence, Felicity gave her sister a triumphant grin. Cecily's sharp single nod accentuated their victory. That would teach Zach to mind his own business.

She wished it meant he would think twice before interjecting his opinions in the future. But it'd be a miracle if that happened. He'd been teasing them as far back as she could remember. He claimed it as his older brother right. But he did it out of love for them. Despite the eight-year span separating the three of them, they were quite close. Felicity hoped that would never change.

"I wonder what type of souvenirs the Chippewa will have for us this year."

"I don't know, Cecily. It will be nice to stroll through the marketplace and browse through their wares."

"I still have that corn-husk doll Father purchased for me seven years ago." Cecily released a melancholic sigh. "It's getting rather worn, though. Perhaps I should see if I can find another to replace it."

The doll sat in a place of honor on top of the cedar chest at the foot of Cecily's bed. A hand-crocheted doily in a circular pattern of thick green and white yarn rested underneath. Although she no longer played with it, it wouldn't be easy for Cecily to part with that doll. Perhaps Mother could find a place to preserve it a little longer.

"I'm certain the dolls will be there, Cecily. They have them every year. I'd like to purchase another reed basket myself. They're woven tighter than the wicker baskets we have back home."

"I'm just hoping they have some big jars of maple sugar," Zach piped in. "Mmm, I can almost taste it."

Felicity laughed. "You'd better have a big jar for your teeth, too, when they rot out of your mouth. You just might single-handedly keep Dr. Wadsworth in business."

"Ha-ha. Very funny." Zach didn't seem too impressed, but he grinned anyway. "I just wish the local fishermen hadn't run John Jacob Astor and his American Fur Company off the island. Although I can't complain about the quality of whitefish and trout they have here. Still, Astor's beaver hats and pelts are some of the finest I've ever owned."

"I agree." Felicity nodded. "Young men look positively dashing in them." She nudged her brother. "Especially you, Zach."

He nudged her in return. "Aw, shucks, sis. You're making me blush."

"There's the docks!" Cecily's voice interrupted their playful banter. Their sister hopped on both feet, leaning over the bow as she pointed into the distance where the hazy outline of the ferry docks came into view.

Mackinac Island. Or Mishla-mackinaw to the local tribes. Even after all these years, the limestone bluffs and high cliffs still amazed her. Excitement surged from within and made Felicity's stomach quiver. She might have protested about coming, but thank goodness Mother didn't concede. Regret surely would have filled her by summer's end.

No sooner had they docked than Cecily grabbed hold of Felicity's arm and almost dragged her off the boat. The crew had just secured the gangplank, and Cecily led the way for all the passengers onto the island. Felicity had no choice. She ran behind her sister, wincing at the amused glances of both their fellow travelers and those who had come to the docks to greet their boat.

"Cecily, slow down!" Felicity tripped on a dip in the dirt path leading up from the docks, then bit her lip when her ankle twisted the wrong way. When she regained her footing, she planted both feet on the ground and yanked Cecily to a stop. Her sister jerked backward and almost ended up on her rear.

"Why did you do a thing like that?" She pulled her hand free from Felicity's and clamped her hands on her tiny waist. "We were almost there."

Felicity lifted her foot an inch or two off the ground and wiggled her ankle back and forth. It seemed all right. No sprain and no evident injury. Raising her gaze to her sister, who stood about a foot above her on the path, she did her best to imitate one of Mother's reproving glares. "Because you were dragging me behind you like we were running from a blazing fire or something equally life-threatening."

Cecily extended her arms out from her sides in a helpless gesture. "I wanted to be the first one to the top." She turned and rushed up the hill, then stood with a triumphant smile stretching from ear to ear.

Felicity climbed the remaining few steps to join her sister and smiled. "And now what are you going to do?"

Her sister looked past Felicity to where Mother and Father and Zach lumbered toward them at a leisurely pace. She shifted her eyes back to Felicity and offered a sheepish grin. "Stand here and wait for the slowpokes?"

With a shake of her head, Felicity turned around to face the rest of their family and snaked her arm around Cecily's waist. A smile she felt clear from her heart found its way to her lips. They were going to have a grand time.

❧

Strains of a stirring Strauss waltz floated down on the breeze that danced over the outdoor raised platform that had been built two years before.

"Are you ready to enjoy an evening of dancing and gaiety and absolutely delicious cuisine?" Zach stood beside her and extended his elbow.

Felicity smiled up at him then lifted her petticoats to prevent any grass stains around the hem. Her brother looked quite dapper in his top hat and tailored suit. Zach's fiancée would no doubt be quite impressed once he joined her family later. For now, Felicity was honored to be escorted by him. She placed her hand in the crook of his arm as they ascended the hill to join the cavorting hotel guests. The elegant men and women dressed in all their finery sat around small white wrought-iron tables surrounding the floor. Larger tables were positioned on the outskirts of the arrangement.

"Mother and Father said they would have a table for us."

Zach nodded. "Yes. They arrived earlier to meet with some friends from previous years."

Perhaps those were the same ones Mother had mentioned yesterday before they left for the train. She was up to something. Felicity just knew it. She and Father both. But what?

"I see them. Over on the far end."

Zach pointed with his right hand to where their parents stood in a circle with a group of people she didn't recognize. At least not from this distance.

"But they're not standing near a table. Which one is ours?"

Zach looked at each empty table between them and their parents. "Aha. That one." He indicated one of the larger ones where Cecily sat, her blond locks curled and styled to perfection. Despite being the only person sitting at the table, she didn't seem the least bit bored. Instead, her attention seemed to be fixated on the energetic couples twirling around the dance floor.

"Let's make our way there, then. Shall we?"

Zach made a grand, sweeping gesture out from his chest. "After you, my lady."

Felicity curtsied. "Why, thank you, my good sir."

She led the way with Zach placing a protective hand at the small of her back. He had become such a fine gentleman in recent years. Mother and Father had raised him well. They'd raised all three of them well. When her brother married and moved into his own home, she'd miss him terribly.

"It's about time you two decided to grace us with your presence."

Zach stepped behind Cecily's chair and reached out to pinch her cheek. She swatted him away and stuck out her tongue. Felicity just rolled her eyes. Some battles simply should not be fought.

"So what types of songs have they played?" Felicity asked, stepping past Cecily.

Zach held Felicity's chair for her and handed his top hat to a waiter before taking a seat opposite, affording all three of them a clear view of the band and the stage.

"Oh, the usual." Cecily ticked off a list on her fingers. "A few waltzes, a new march by Sousa, and a piece from Rossini."

"There will no doubt be some pieces from Mozart, Beethoven, Verdi, and Wagner throughout the evening as well."

Zach winked at both Cecily and Felicity. "I see the tutelage Mother insisted you two undergo has proven itself rather useful."

"Culture and a solid grasp of the musical greats are essential to any young woman's successful upbringing." Felicity gave her brother a pointed look. "It would do you good to familiarize yourself with these masters of music as well." She grinned. "Especially if you are ever going to impress your fiancée. How you managed to convince her to marry you, I'll never know."

Cecily giggled and covered her mouth with her gloved hand. Felicity held Zach's gaze and engaged him in a visual duel. He held his own and leaned forward, his forearm resting on the edge of the table.

"If you are so concerned about suitable marriage liaisons,

then you should be worrying about your own." He leaned back in his chair and interlaced his fingers behind his head. "You'll soon be twenty. I daresay Mother and Father have already taken the necessary steps toward finding you a suitable husband."

"Be that as it may," Felicity retorted, "Father has assured me that he will not enter into any official agreement without my advance knowledge of the young gentleman's identity or my agreement to the union."

"I eagerly anticipate the day I have the good fortune to meet the young man who is worthy of your affections. With your standards set so high, it's going to have to be a man worth his salt to meet them."

Brandt could do it. The thought came unbidden, and Felicity shook it from her head. Mackinac Island society and this entire experience were as far away as she could get from Brandt and the temporary world in which she lived. She had to put him out of her mind.

Felicity changed her position and modified her posture, turning away from Zach and tilting her chin in the air. "There is absolutely nothing wrong with having high standards. It will guarantee me the perfect match. If a young man is unwilling to meet those standards or I find him lacking in certain areas, I shall know he isn't the right man for me."

"At least you're old enough to be giving marriage a serious thought," Cecily mumbled. "Father said I still have three more years." She stuck out her lower lip.

Felicity glanced at Zach, his eyes full of mirth and his lips turning white from holding back his laughter. She almost laughed as well, but it wouldn't help her sister any.

"Don't be in such a rush, Cecily." Felicity reached over and placed her hand on her sister's arm. "Your time will come. Choosing the one who will share the rest of your life is no decision to take lightly. Besides," she said as she leaned away again and grinned, "whoever this man is, he'll not only have to pass Mother and Father's approval, but Zach's and mine as well."

"That's right," Zach chimed in. "And I don't know how keen I am about some young lad stealing away my baby sister."

That did it—they'd been successful at getting their sister's mind off the grumbling. Cecily placed both hands flat on the table and hopped her gaze between the two of them.

"By the time I'm ready to consider marriage, the two of you will likely have married and settled with a spouse of your own. So I will have nothing to worry about."

"Excuse me, Miss Chambers, but would you honor me with a dance?"

All three of them stopped and stared at a well-dressed young man who stood next to Cecily with one gloved hand extended palm up in her direction.

Cecily didn't waste a second. She placed her hand in his and allowed him to help her to her feet. A moment later the young man led Cecily onto the floor and into a smooth waltz.

"Wasn't that—?"

Felicity nodded. "Yes. I do believe that was Matthew Lodge." She stared at Matthew and Cecily as they glided across the floor. "My, but he's become quite a handsome young man since last we saw him."

"I wonder if Mother and Father are aware of this development."

Zach looked across the table at Felicity, and she looked back at him.

She smiled. "Are you thinking what I'm thinking?"

Her brother stood in haste and came around the table,

then bowed. "Would you do me the honor, Miss Chambers, of joining me in this waltz?"

Felicity accepted his invitation and hurried alongside him as they waited for the right moment to merge with the other couples. They might not be able to speak to Matthew Lodge, but at least they could keep an eye on him and their sister.

After two complete sets, Matthew escorted Cecily back to their family's table and bowed over her hand. Cecily nodded with a smile. Zach led Felicity toward them, but she couldn't make out their words. Before they reached their seats, Matthew left.

Felicity placed her hands on the back of her chair. "Did you two have a nice time?"

The smile hadn't left Cecily's lips. "A wonderful one."

Zach took on the older brother role and leveled a warning glance at Cecily. "Well, he'd better be sure to treat you with the utmost respect, or I might have a few words with him."

"Don't be silly, Zach. Matthew did nothing improper. In fact, he—"

"Felicity," Mother's voice interrupted. "I'm so glad to see you've returned from dancing. Your father and I would like to introduce you to someone."

Felicity looked across the table at Zach, who only raised his eyebrows as if to say, "I told you so."

"He comes from a fine, upstanding family," Mother continued, completely oblivious. "And his father has several long-standing investments in the mining and refinery businesses."

So this is what Mother had meant when she said she and Father had been working hard on something. Why did they feel the need to be so secretive? Why not come right out and tell her what they were planning? Felicity wanted nothing to do with Mother and Father's matchmaking schemes. But she owed it to them to at least pretend to go along.

She took a deep breath and turned to face the unknown man. "Felicity Chambers, I'd like to introduce you to—"

"Brandt!"

twelve

The single word had escaped Felicity's mouth before she could stop it. What was Brandt doing here? And dressed in those clothes? She had managed to see him briefly before her last day at the factory. He'd said he had to go out of town for a few days but would see her upon his return. She didn't have time to tell him she'd be gone as well. Despite the timing being rather vague and parallel to her own itinerary, she hadn't given it much thought. She never would have guessed that journey would bring him here to Mackinac Island!

Mother's gasp sounded distant to Felicity's ears. She'd thought of Brandt several times that day, wishing he could be there with her and see the island. Now here he stood, dressed in a fine, tailored suit with tails on his outer jacket. He looked every bit as out of place as if Timothy, Mrs. Gibson's oldest son, had appeared before her eyes dressed in similar fashion.

"Have you two already been introduced?"

"In a manner of speaking, yes," Brandt said.

She saw his lips move, but she still couldn't seem to make sense of it all. Considering the circumstances, Felicity expected shock from Brandt. Instead, his eyes held a diverse blend of curiosity, anger, hurt, and impatience. Felicity knew the feelings well. Each one of them churned inside her, too. He no doubt had put two and two together when he'd been introduced to her parents. But still, he accompanied them here to meet her and maintain the ruse. Why? So many questions begged to be answered. So many thoughts fought for dominance.

But worst of all, Brandt now knew her secret.

"Felicity, dear, are you all right? Your skin is so pale. Harold, come take a look. I don't believe our daughter is feeling well."

"Davinia, what is it?"

Brandt didn't move. He didn't flinch. His eyes held hers, and she couldn't break the powerful hold. Activity and movement occurred around her, but she didn't hear what they were saying. Then her father's deep voice penetrated through her consciousness.

"If we had known you two were already acquainted, the Lawsons and your mother and I could've saved a lot of time."

Father's words snapped the invisible rope tying Felicity's gaze to Brandt's. A spark flashed in Brandt's eyes, and Felicity shook her head. Her muscles moved like molasses as she turned to face her parents. She did her best to maintain control. "Do you mean to say that you have been planning this meeting for some time now?"

"And that you made all the arrangements behind our backs, without bothering to consult either one of us?" Brandt directed his question at his own parents.

"It seemed like the perfect opportunity, Felicity," Mother offered. "Mr. Lawson came to call one afternoon, and we invited him to share tea with us. Having heard of his tremendous success in the mining industry, your father and I were intrigued about the purpose of his visit."

Father placed his arm around his wife and nodded. "What he had to say surprised us both."

Mr. Lawson—not Dalton as she'd assumed from Brandt's story—looked back and forth between his son and Felicity before settling his attention on his son. "When we spoke a few weeks ago about your progress at the refinery, Brandt, you mentioned Miss Chambers and provided her full name to me."

"If I had known what you would do with that information, I never would have said a word."

Fury seemed to seethe from between his words. Felicity couldn't see his eyes, but as the sound of his voice indicated, the storm brewing inside wouldn't remain contained much longer. Thankfully the band music and clamor of conversations among the other guests drowned out the argument between the two families. For the moment, Brandt at least appeared to have pushed his reaction to her ruse to the side. But the time for that confrontation would come all too soon.

"Now, Brandt," Mr. Lawson continued, his voice calm. He raised one hand, no doubt in an attempt to stay his son's anger. "If you focused more on the practical aspect of these proceedings instead of your irritation, you'll come to see just how providential all this is."

"I'm listening." Brandt said the words, but his tone indicated otherwise.

Felicity didn't know whether to get involved or remain a bystander. She should be planning what she'd say to Brandt when the revelation of their respective subterfuges came to a head. They both had their own reasons for doing what they did, but the fact that their parents had gotten involved in this as well made Felicity want to run away from it all.

Morbid curiosity made her stay.

Mr. Lawson relaxed, the harsh lines in his forehead fading and his shoulders dropping an inch or two. "Very good." He took a deep breath and glanced around the small area where they stood before seeking out Felicity's parents. "Would we not be more comfortable sitting down for this? I daresay the other guests here would find the details of our conversation a bit less interesting if we weren't providing such a public demonstration for them."

"That's a splendid idea," Father agreed.

Oh yes. Have everyone sit down. That way the situation wouldn't seem as serious. But it *was* serious. If only Brandt would look at her. Offer some sort of sign that they were in this together against their parents. She might not be so confused.

Felicity's heart pounded and blood rushed to her head, the steady beat against her temples making it difficult to concentrate. She closed her eyes for a moment, and when she opened them again, Mother's arm came around her shoulders and compelled her to follow Father, who guided the little entourage to a less conspicuous location.

As Felicity walked by her brother and sister still sitting at the family table, they offered sympathetic expressions. But even their support did little to diminish the frustration of being a pawn in her parents' plans.

Once everyone was seated, Felicity attempted to get Brandt's attention, but he refused to look at her. She sat in the middle of her parents, with Brandt on the other side of Father and the Lawsons on the other side of Mother. Mrs. Lawson hadn't said a single word since all this had started. But Brandt hadn't mentioned her much, either. If she was like most society women Felicity knew, she stayed out of conflicts like these. Felicity wished she could do the same.

Mr. Lawson continued, his attention again focused on Brandt.

"Now as I said, you gave me Miss Chambers's name that day. From the way you spoke of her, I could see there were feelings you refused to admit to me. Because of the nature of the position you held, being on the cusp of assuming such integral responsibilities at my factories, I knew something had to be done."

"And so you took it upon yourself to solve the world's problems as you saw fit." Derision laced each word Brandt spoke.

"You left me with little choice in the matter."

"Whatever happened to trusting me to make the right choice and giving me the benefit of the doubt?"

Now that exchange sounded familiar. Felicity had an almost identical one with her parents the first time she had mentioned Brandt's name. Only that time the results had been much more favorable.

"As I watched you each day for almost three weeks, I noticed a change. I believed your emotions were too deeply intertwined for rational decisions to be made." His gaze shifted to encompass both Mother and Father, and he offered a slight smile. "Besides, when I learned the true identity of Miss Chambers and her lineage, I couldn't have been more pleased."

Mother beamed and Father nodded his appreciation of the compliment. But they remained silent. Perhaps they had all four agreed beforehand who would carry the conversation when their plan was revealed. Still, Felicity wished her parents would say something or that Brandt would stop acting like she wasn't even there.

Mr. Lawson continued. "I withheld the fact that you were already acquainted with Felicity and instead sought out a plan for an introduction in your more familiar settings. After further discussion, we all learned we'd be here on the island simultaneously, and it seemed like the perfect opportunity."

Brandt waved his arm out over the table in the direction of his father. "And rather than coming to me to discuss it further, you made my decisions for me."

"Let's not become irrational about this." Father spoke up for the first time since all of them sat down. "We can discuss this in a calm manner."

Mother started to speak, but Father placed his hand over hers, and she closed her mouth, clasping her hands in her lap.

Brandt turned his attention to Father and took a deep breath. "I don't mean any disrespect, Mr. Chambers, but this situation is beyond calm and rational. I don't exactly like the idea of being someone's puppet," he said, swerving his gaze back to his father, "to be controlled at will."

Mr. Lawson acted rather satisfied with what he'd done. No evidence of any regret or remorse could be found in his expression. "You seemed to indicate that Miss Chambers was nothing more than a friend. A passing acquaintance. I didn't see any harm in orchestrating circumstances which might produce more desirable results."

Brandt jumped to his feet, overturning his chair and sending it skidding back a few feet behind him. Fire flashed in his eyes. Mother and Mrs. Lawson gasped. Father started to retrieve the chair only to be intercepted by a watchful waiter standing nearby.

"My relationship with Miss Chambers, whatever it may be," Brandt fumed, "is between Miss Chambers and myself. No one else." He extended his hand, palm up. "What you've done"—his arm moved to encompass both sets of parents— "what you've *all* done is beyond excusable. You should never have interfered."

Felicity had never seen Brandt so angry. If he was this upset about their parents' covert schemes, how much more so would he be with her for her deception? She didn't want to wait to find out.

"I'm sorry," she spoke up, her voice coming out more like a squeak. Hot liquid gathered in her eyes, blurring the faces before her. "I can't bear to listen to any more of this. I. . .I must go."

Before anyone could object, she pushed back her chair, gathered her skirts, and fled the scene. Cries from those gathered at the table reached her ears, but she paid them no mind. The only voice she waited for was Brandt's. Despite the fear of what would happen when the parts they played in this manipulative maneuvering were brought to light, his voice was the only one she wanted to hear.

"Felicity, wait!"

And there it was. But she was too far gone to stop now. Blinded by the rivulets streaming down her face, she half ran, half stumbled down the hill toward the water. She vaguely recalled a gazebo set back a little from the lakeshore. Glancing up at the crescent-shaped moon, she prayed she headed in the right direction. Clomping footsteps sounded behind her, but she didn't stop. Brushing her hand across her eyes to clear some of the tears, Felicity trudged onward. The ethereal glow of the gazebo drew her, its outline illuminated by the waning quarter moon above.

Just as she reached the entrance, a hand grabbed her arm.

"Felicity, please," Brandt huffed, his breathing labored and uneven.

"No, Brandt." She shook off his hand and reached for the railing. "Please. Leave me alone." Tripping up the stairs and giving no thought to soiling her gown, she crumpled in a heap in front of the nearest bench, burying her head in the circle of her arms on the bench's surface. Sporadic sobs escaped her lips as more tears fell from her eyes.

The bottom of Brandt's shoes clacked on the pine steps, and the silky fabric of his tailored suit rustled as he joined her inside. His leg brushed against her arm as he took a seat on the bench. A warm hand touched her shoulder. She wanted to welcome his comfort, allow him to console her. But she couldn't.

For all of his words defending their actions to their parents, she had still deceived him. He had withheld the truth, too, and the acknowledgment of that had to come out.

❧

Brandt didn't know whether to shake her or put his arms around her and pull her close. He'd never really learned to handle a woman's tears. Coming from Felicity, though, it showed at least a hint of remorse and brokenness over the whole crazy situation.

She'd also never looked so beautiful, with her hair piled on top of her head and the elegant gown hugging her slender frame. The dresses she wore to work didn't do her justice. She looked born to wear gowns like this.

He raked his fingers through his hair, feeling the well-groomed strands stand on end. How had things gotten so out of hand?

One minute he was laughing and spending time with friends, and the next he was squaring off against his parents, facing the consequences of his actions.

"Felicity, will you at least look at me?"

"No," came the muffled sob.

"Fine." He slapped his hands on his thighs and stood. "Then I guess there's no reason for me to stay." He took two steps and stopped when he heard her voice.

"Wait."

He turned to face her.

Felicity raised her head and used her fingers to wipe her eyes. For several moments she sat there, not moving or saying anything. Then she placed her palms on the bench and rose from the floor of the gazebo to sit on the bench in the spot he'd just vacated.

Her head remained downcast. She worried the folds of her gown as she mustered up what he guessed were the words she wanted to say. He waited as she lifted her chin and presented tear-soaked eyes to him.

"Why did you not tell me the truth?" she pleaded in a soft voice.

Brandt slapped his hand against his chest, where a shot of indignation burned. "Why didn't *I* tell the truth? What about you?" He made a sweeping gesture of his hand toward her.

"The façade *you* presented, working for Mrs. Gibson in the factory and withholding the part about your social status, wasn't exactly honest, either."

Felicity's fingers curled around the edge of the bench where she sat. "I was doing charity work for Lucy. And I didn't see the need to reveal that much information."

He leaned against the post at the entrance and folded his arms. "Charity work that would add another notch to your good service belt, no doubt."

The second he cast the words out on the wind, Brandt wanted to reel them back. But it was too late.

She gasped and recoiled against one of the whitewashed pine support beams. Her lower lip trembled before she got it under control. "At least what I did and do is out of goodness for those in need. You were misrepresenting yourself to the other men at the refinery. I assume your father owns the refinery, and the only goal you had in mind was the lofty ambition of one day taking over control of the operation."

"Yes, Father does own the refinery. I was learning the way that operation works so I could better understand all aspects before I was put in charge. And I wasn't allowed to reveal who I was. That," he said, leveling a pointed look at her, "was my father's mandate. I merely obeyed and adapted as needed."

"Creatively disguising your true identity so the men working side by side with you wouldn't know they were working with their soon-to-be boss." Her lips trembled, as if she were trying to conceal her hurt, and her words came out choked. "How thoughtful of you."

"Look." He planted both feet on the pine planks beneath him and lowered his arms. "I had no control over what my father required me to do."

"But you *did* have control regarding what you said and to whom," she pointed out.

"Yes, but I couldn't come right out and tell everyone who I was. Father would have found out, and I could have risked my entire future."

"You could have been honest with some."

"And risk those choice people telling someone else? That would've been taking too big a chance. There were consequences either way." He shifted his weight. "Take you, for example. Had I told you who I was from the start, you likely would have never believed me."

This time it was her turn to cross her arms in a defensive manner. "And what makes you come to that conclusion?"

"Think about how I was dressed. There wasn't time to explain the whole situation since I was already late for my first day on the job. And the next day? Anything I said would have sounded false."

"So instead of being honest, you chose what you felt was the easier path and led me to believe you were something you're not."

Brandt nodded. "Exactly the same thing you did to me."

"I—" She opened her mouth then clamped it shut as she stared at him.

He inwardly gloated that she didn't have an immediate retort. He grew tired of this seemingly endless verbal battle anyway. He'd just told her his reasoning. She should do the same.

"Why did *you* feign the truth to the girls in the factory and act like someone *you* weren't?"

She stiffened as her chin jutted upward an inch. Great. So now he'd wounded her pride in addition to angering her. At least they were on even ground.

"Because I didn't want any of them to feel awkward around me or treat me any differently simply because my family had wealth. Working there afforded me a sense of independence. For once I didn't have to concern myself with someone else controlling every aspect of my life. I and I alone decided."

"Did you also decide what you would do when someone discovered your ruse?"

"No. It wasn't going to last long. By the time it became an issue, I would have moved on to other work. But that's neither here nor there. My work at the factory is done."

Brandt pushed off from the post and started to pace. Done? Just like that? She made it sound so trivial. He had become the alter ego because Father demanded it. He had lied, but out of necessity. Now he had to pay the piper for his actions. She had lied as well, but she didn't seem to think it meant a great deal.

"Had you ever planned to confess to anyone?"

"I hadn't thought that far ahead."

He snorted. "That's obvious."

"Why are you so angry at me? It's not like I'm the only one in the wrong here."

She had a lot of nerve asking him that. He stopped in the center of the gazebo. "Why am I angry?"

"Yes."

"Because you didn't trust me, that's why."

Felicity uncrossed her arms and instead planted them on her hips. "Trust you with what?"

"The fact that you came from money." He resumed pacing. "Did you think I'd treat you differently if I knew? That I'd suddenly want to be a friend and get to know you only for your wealth?"

"How should I know?"

"Well, I was nothing more than a refinery worker," he said, flailing one arm wildly in the air. "And the working class doesn't socialize with the upper classes."

She dropped her hands to rest on each side of her legs. "That was exactly the reason I *did* agree to our friendship. You were a refreshing change from the boorish men I knew."

He paused again. That was a switch Brandt didn't see coming. Why couldn't she stick to the topic at hand without changing it again? He had a hard enough time keeping up with the direction of the conversation without her added course alterations.

She continued. "And of course, Mother and Father warned me against it."

"Well, they didn't see what you saw. They only knew I wasn't good enough for you."

She shrugged. "Not as Brandt Dalton, no. But you were as Brandt Lawson."

Brandt paused a moment. Could she be softening a bit, or could his imagination be playing tricks on him?

"The same goes for my father. That is, until he found out who *you* really were."

"And if you hadn't given him my full name, he never would have known, and we wouldn't be in this mess right now."

Great. There went another twist. How did she manage to know just the right words to cut straight to the heart? He crossed his arms again, lest she shoot another piercing remark his way.

"So now this is *my* fault? How did we get back to blaming me again?"

"Not you so much as your father." Felicity's eyes narrowed. "But now that you mention it, you did go along with him. No questions asked."

"He's my father. And I respect him. What else did you expect me to do?"

"You could have found an alternate path to take that wouldn't have been so deceptive or come with so much potential hurt for others."

"And the same goes for you."

She sighed. Her eyelids slowly closed then opened again. "So where does this leave us now?"

A guttural groan rumbled inside him and found its way to his mouth. "I don't know."

"We can't undo what we've done, nor can we go back to the way we were, now that we know the truth."

Did she have to put it in such plain language and state it in such a matter-of-fact manner? As if he didn't already know.

"I think we both just need to go away for a while." Wait a minute. He couldn't presume to speak for her. "No, *I* need to go away. To sort a few things out."

Had he really just said that?

"That sounds like an. . .excellent idea."

The catch in her voice drew his attention to her face. Stone-hardened indifference. That was all he saw. No, wait. A trace of hopelessness and regret also lingered. Could she actually be wishing for a different outcome? One that didn't require them to go their separate ways?

"I think we could both benefit from the time alone," she said.

There went that idea. Obviously she wasn't as broken up over his leaving as he thought. It wasn't as though he wanted it to be this way. So how did she make him feel like it was all his decision? He really did need to put some distance between them. Because if he didn't throttle her, he'd crush her against his chest and never let her go.

Dropping an invisible shield between them, Brandt took three steps and stood in the doorway of the gazebo. For a brief second that regret returned again, and he almost reconsidered. He had to leave now. For both their sakes.

"Very well, Miss Chambers." He bowed and bid her farewell. "I hope you enjoy the remainder of your time here on the island. Good night."

With that he did an about-face and fled, taking long strides and getting away from her as fast as his slippery shoes would take him. There would be time for regret later.

thirteen

"I can't believe you never told me about him."

Cecily picked up a corn-husk doll and examined it before setting it back in place. Felicity walked beside her sister as they browsed the souvenirs in the open-air marketplace. Local Cherokee were there along with various vendors from Mackinaw City. It was their last day on the island, and Felicity wanted nothing more than to get on the train and return to her normal life back in Detroit. Only it wouldn't be normal. Everything would be different now that her ruse had come to light. She no longer had her work at the factory where she could escape.

"I never saw the need to mention him." And Felicity regretted that decision. Perhaps if she had been honest with her sister, some of this hurt could have been avoided. She ran her fingers over several meticulously crafted quill boxes. She had her reed basket. Now she wanted something more special.

"Ooh! This one is perfect!" Cecily almost draped herself across the table reaching for what seemed like the hundredth doll that morning. "It's almost a perfect replica of the one Father purchased all those years ago."

She bartered a moment or two with the woman at the table, then retrieved some coins and paid for her doll. Cecily held her shoulders a bit higher after making that purchase, yet continued to browse the tables. Felicity followed behind.

"So you meet a handsome young man and spend time with him. And you don't see the need to speak about him to your only sister?" Cecily stopped and turned. "You might think I'm too young to understand all this. But I'd say you either wanted to keep him to yourself or you were afraid of what Mother or Father might say when they found out." She poked Felicity in the shoulder. "Now you know."

Felicity took a step forward and the two started walking again. "But that's just it, Cecily. I *don't* know."

"What do you mean?"

"All I know from Mother and Father is they approve of Brandt Lawson, and they were planning behind my back to arrange an introduction in the hopes that we might form a union together." And if she had met Brandt for the first time under those circumstances, that might have been a possibility. But now? "When Mother and Father learned about Brandt Dalton, they warned me against any liaisons with him."

Cecily shrugged. "That's because they only knew him as a refinery worker. And that would never do. Now, though, he's the heir to his father's holdings. I don't see the problem. You obviously have their blessing."

"He lied to me, Cecily." Felicity adjusted the handles of the reed basket on her arm. "How will I ever know I can trust him again?"

Casting a look over her shoulder, Cecily's lips formed a rueful line. "Don't forget you lied to him, too. He's probably wondering if he can trust you as well."

"Yes, you're right." What a mess she'd made of things. She hadn't intended for anyone to get hurt. But it was too late for that. She and Brandt both had been wrong. Felicity sighed. "I don't know if we can move past this."

"Have you thought of prayer? You used to tell me all the time it was the answer to all my problems. When I didn't know what to do, I should talk to God. Aside from that, the lies are something the two of you are going to have to work out yourselves."

It sounded so simple yet so complex. Amazing how the perspective of someone younger could actually shed light on her quandary. Felicity draped her arm around her sister's shoulders.

"You know, for a child you're rather intelligent."

Cecily gave her a smug grin. "I know. I had an excellent teacher."

Felicity shook her head and chuckled. Despite her mistakes and errors in judgment, her sister still admired her. That proved God hadn't left her alone to fix this dilemma. Sunlight glinted off something shiny just ahead, and she picked up her pace, almost dragging her sister with her. At the sight of the beautiful handcrafted items on the small stand, Felicity froze.

The seller stood next to the display in a tailored suit, his hands clasping the lapels of his coat as he rocked back and forth on his heels. He raised one hand to smooth the thin lines of his short mustache with his thumb and forefinger.

"These pieces are exquisitely crafted jeweled eggs. Each one is unique. No two are alike." He selected one and held it out. "Please. Take a look for yourself."

Cecily pressed against her side. "Oh, Felicity, it's stunning."

Felicity took the item in her hands and observed it from all angles. She ran her fingers across the etchings on the outside and marveled at the intricate detail of the artwork. An entire piece made of gold and clear crystal gem pieces.

The top held a single gemstone surrounded by what appeared to be the roof of a rotunda. Below, a pattern of gold draping tied with bows at the pinnacle left openings in the egg to reveal a small gift box tucked inside. Underneath the bows two sections of scrollwork fashioned after flowers with flowing stems and vines circled the perimeter against a background of pearl-like marble. A hinge connected the two parts. Directly opposite the hinge sat a clasp with a gemstone that duplicated the one on top. The egg sat on a stem that had been welded together and had four oval pearls, one on each side, which gave way to the fanned-out base.

"Do forgive me for interrupting your admiration of the piece, miss, but may I?"

Felicity tore her attention away from the decorative item to look at the seller. "Pardon me?"

"If you will permit me to show you this one thing." He reached for the clasp and opened it. "As an added bonus, there is also a musical melody that plays."

"Ooh!" Cecily clapped her hands. "It's just like a music box."

Felicity stared at the little box as it slowly spun while the tune played.

"Oh, Felicity, you simply must get this one. It will look wonderful next to the handcrafted items in your curio cabinet."

This item had to be costly. The etchings alone must have taken hours. And the intricacies of the designs as well as the music box feature had to raise the price even more.

"How much are you selling these for?"

"Seven dollars and two bits."

Felicity's throat tightened. That amount was more than she had with her. But the piece was so beautiful. She had only to find Father, and it would be hers.

"To own one of these will make you the envy of all your friends. And the value of them will only continue to increase as time passes."

He made it sound so appealing. Could she justify such an extravagant purchase, though? Especially when she knew people like Mrs. Gibson or even Laura and Brianna were unable to afford the basics of life, much less luxuries like this? No. There were far better uses of her abundance than to spend it on another frivolity to add to her collection.

She handed the egg back to the seller, and her shoulders slumped. "Thank you, sir, but I do believe I must decline. Perhaps another time."

The seller bowed. "I shall be here for the remainder of the summer and will likely return again next season." Reaching into an inner pocket of his suit, the man withdrew a small white card. "Should you desire to contact me at any other time, this is my calling card."

Felicity took it from him and tucked it into her handbag. "Thank you very much for allowing me the time to admire your fine collection. We wish you much success."

He nodded. "Good day, ladies."

Cecily remained silent until they had walked about fifteen feet from the stand; then she wrapped her hand around Felicity's upper arm and leaned close. "I can't believe you didn't buy it. What's the matter with you?"

"Life isn't just about buying the things you want, Cecily. Sometimes there are more important matters."

"And I think all that charity work and your time spent at the factory have warped your sensibilities."

"Perhaps."

"No wonder the young men who live in Grosse Pointe never caught your attention and you fell for Brandt as a refinery worker."

Her sister's remark made her pause. Is that why she had found Brandt so appealing? Because as Brandt Dalton he was different from any other man she'd met? She brushed aside those thoughts for another time when she could analyze them at greater length.

"Shall we make our way back to the beginning? I believe I saw some lovely porcupine quill boxes, and I believe I'll purchase one of them to go with this reed basket."

"Very well."

Cecily's enthusiasm seemed diminished, but Felicity refused to take the blame. If her sister had loved the piece so much, she should have bought it. For now it would remain a nice memory of her visit here this summer.

As they passed the display again, Felicity dipped her head in response to the seller's nod. Movement behind the man drew her gaze just up the hill.

Brandt!

Her disloyal heart leapt at the sight of him. Her head told her to keep walking. How long had he been standing there? Was he following her? He was the one who had first said he needed some time away. Surely he could find somewhere else on the island to be. She tried to ignore his presence, but her mind refused to cooperate.

The sooner they returned home, the better.

❧

Pain-filled screams reached Felicity's ears the minute she turned the corner on her way to Mrs. Gibson's.

The baby!

She ran past the first two homes and burst through the front door of the Gibson home. Her eyes searched the room. Marianne kneeled beside Lucy, a wet cloth pressed to the woman's forehead.

"The pains just started," the younger girl said. "I was about to fetch the doctor."

Lucy had a death grip on the back and bottom front of the couch where she lay. Her five children were all absent. They'd likely gone to a neighbor's or friend's house.

Felicity had to do something. She'd never seen a baby being born. She'd heard the midwife took care of that. If they were back at her home, she'd send a servant for the doctor or call for a buggy to take Mrs. Gibson to the hospital. But here? She didn't know the first thing to do.

Movement around the corner caught her eye, and she looked toward the other room.

"Timothy!"

The lad jumped back, losing his balance and landing on his backside. After he scrambled to his feet, he brushed oily hair in need of a wash and a trim out of his eyes and assumed an uneven stance. "You need something, Miss Felicity?"

God bless the helpful boy.

"Yes, Timothy. I need you to fetch the doctor. You know your mother's going to have her baby, and I'm worried there might be trouble. We're going to need the doctor's help."

Timothy squared his shoulders and slapped his right hand over his heart. "You can count on me, Miss Felicity."

"Go as fast as you can, Timothy. Run!"

The boy stumbled a bit getting started, but as soon as he reached the street, he took off. Felicity smiled. That boy was going to make a fine man when he grew up. She went back inside and immediately to Mrs. Gibson.

"Marianne, why don't you prepare some nourishment for Mrs. Gibson? As soon as Timothy returns with the doctor, Mrs. Gibson might need something to give her strength."

Marianne nodded and stood. "I'll set some broth to heat and fetch some cold water." She stood and backed away, wringing her hands on her apron. "I'm real sorry I didn't send Timothy sooner, Miss Felicity. But someone had to be here with the missus."

Felicity offered a reassuring smile. "You did everything just fine, Marianne. Now pray the doctor arrives soon and tend to the tasks you mentioned."

Just twenty minutes later, the door swung open and Timothy ran inside, a stern-looking man with a medical bag following close on his heels. He quickly assessed the situation, dropped his cap on the chair in the corner, and went to kneel at Lucy's side.

"Has she been screaming long? Have you been keeping her cooled down? Do you have extra blankets and boiling water ready? How far apart are the contractions?"

Contractions? Water? Blankets? Felicity sat back on her haunches, dumbfounded.

The doctor's stern expression softened some as he glanced at her. "How often does she feel the intense pain?"

"Oh!" Contractions. Yes, she understood those. "Every four or five minutes, I believe."

He rolled up his sleeves and dug into his medical bag for a few instruments. Most she didn't recognize, but the stethoscope she knew. He set the two ends in his ears then placed the round piece over Lucy's abdomen and listened.

"Everything sounds just fine, Mrs. Gibson." He placed a hand on her forehead and smiled. Lucy returned a weak smile, her eyes half closed and perspiration dotting her upper lip.

Felicity closed her eyes and prayed everything would go smoothly. *God, we really do need Your divine assistance this day.* Lucy had been through so much this past year. Losing a husband in a boating accident was enough for any woman. She shouldn't have to lose this baby, too.

"Miss Chambers, I'm going to need you to assist me. Are you feeling up to it?"

She almost said she wasn't, but Lucy needed her. "Yes, Doctor. I'll do whatever you need."

"All right. Go into the kitchen and boil a pot of water. Then gather as many blankets as you can from around the house." He lifted the dented metal bowl from the floor. "Dump this out and fill it with fresh cold water. Then bring some extra cloths for keeping her cool."

"Right away, Doctor."

In no time at all, the squalling baby entered the world, and as far as Felicity could tell, without complications. She raised her eyes to the ceiling and smiled.

"Heavenly Father, thank You."

"Amen to that!" came the doctor's hearty reply. He held the baby over a makeshift table by the wall, using the now hot water to wash the newborn. A minute later, he swaddled the child and made his way back to Lucy. "I could never do what I do without His help," he said, kneeling beside the couch.

Felicity peered over the doctor's shoulder. The infant squirmed and fidgeted within its confines. Only whimpers escaped the tiny lips as the doctor settled the baby into Lucy's waiting arms with a smile.

"Mrs. Gibson, you have yourself another healthy baby girl."

The wonder and the joy of life. A miracle in and of itself. Lucy seemed so peaceful now, and the little girl seemed to know her mother now held her. What had begun as heartache and loss for Lucy now ended in wonder and delight. The circle was now complete.

Before long Lucy would be back on her feet and able to work again at the factory. She'd be well on her way toward providing for her family again. That realization brought sudden sadness. Where did that leave Felicity? These past few months had been the longest of any charity service she'd performed. It already felt odd knowing everything was about to change. What would happen when that day actually arrived?

Felicity needed to start thinking more about that. She didn't want to find herself at the end of this current phase without a plan for the next. Today marked the beginning of the end. She truly would miss all of this.

≈

Brandt stared at the figures in the three columns for the eighth time. They refused to add up. He must be missing something.

He'd been overseeing the work at the refinery for almost a month, and this was the first time he'd had a problem focusing. He didn't want to admit that it might have something to do with catching a glimpse of Felicity earlier when he was outside on his lunch break.

He'd made some well-placed inquiries and learned that Mrs. Gibson had delivered a healthy baby girl the day after he'd returned from Mackinac. She'd been deemed fit to return to work this week. He was glad Mrs. Gibson had recovered, but her return only solidified Felicity's absence. He'd been to the candle factory to discuss business with the manager there at least once a week during the past month, and he'd never seen Felicity. She told him she had quit before the visit to the island. But then why had she returned today?

They hadn't spoken since that fateful day in August. And as he'd figured, the time away from her had helped clear his head.

Today, though, no manner of figures or mindless tasks could take his thoughts away from Felicity. He tried going for a walk, but he only saw the places where they'd talked and shared a picnic. Back in the office, the four walls seemed to close in around him.

Brandt grabbed his coat off the back of the chair. "I need to go home."

After stomping down the back stairs, he shoved the door open with a bang and thudded into the street. All the way home he brooded. How had she managed to bewitch him? Why couldn't he get her out of his mind? He should be worrying about facts and figures and new equipment. Not getting stuck on the image of one girl.

"Master Lawson, sir." Jeffrey opened the front door just as Brandt reached the landing out front. "It's a surprise to see you home so early, sir. Is everything all right at work?"

Brandt shed his coat and dumped it into his butler's arms. "Everything at work is fine, Jeffrey." He jabbed his index finger against the side of his head. "It's up here that there's a problem."

Jeffrey gave him a puzzled look. "Your head, sir? Are you ill? Do you need me to fetch the doctor, sir?"

If Brandt hadn't been so frustrated, he might have chuckled at Jeffrey's concern. If only a doctor could fix this.

"No, Jeffrey. I'm not ill. And no, I don't need the doctor. What I *do* need is a tall glass of lemonade and—"

"And your rather worn copy of *Journey to the Center of the Earth*, perhaps?"

He smiled. How well Jeffrey knew him. If he couldn't be somewhere listening to a band play some of his favorite music, he'd rather be inside with a book by Jules Verne—no matter how many times he'd read it.

"That would be perfect, Jeffrey. Thank you."

"As you wish, sir."

"And Jeffrey?"

"Yes, sir?"

"What did I tell you about the 'sir' business?"

Jeffrey bowed with a half smirk on his lips. "As you wish." He hung up Brandt's coat and disappeared down the hall toward the kitchen.

Brandt made his way to the library. The dark interior welcomed him with the familiar smells of leather, paper, and the ever-present pipe tobacco. He sank into the plush leather seat and propped his feet on the footstool in front of him.

His butler reappeared a moment later with the requested items and placed the glass on the table next to the chair.

"Will there be anything else?"

"No, Jeffrey. That's all for now. Thank you."

"Very well. I shall inform your mother that you're home.

I believe she wishes to speak with you."

Brandt nodded as Jeffrey exited into the hallway, leaving the door open to let some light in. What did Mother want to discuss with him? Usually Father had an agenda in mind. But if his mother had something to say, now would be the perfect time. Father wouldn't be there to interrupt.

He waited for ten minutes, but she didn't come. Perhaps he should get some reading done in the interim. He lit a lamp on the small table beside him. As tradition had it, once he settled in for a good read, Mother would interrupt.

Flipping open the well-worn cover, Brandt slid his fingers on the edges of the pages as he turned them. He reached the first page and refreshed his memory about the professor and his family.

Sure enough, as he reached page five Mother's silhouette appeared outlined by the light from the hall. Brandt slapped the book closed and tucked it against his thigh. This likely wouldn't last long. Mother wasn't one to beat around the bush.

"Brandt," she began as she came farther into the study, "I have been meaning to speak with you before now. But the opportunity hadn't presented itself."

He smirked to himself. Exactly as he predicted. She didn't bother with any formalities.

"By all means, Mother." He rested his hands on his thighs. "I'm listening."

Mother approached until she stood directly in front of him. She opened her mouth to speak, then paused. A moment later, she tried again. "Why are you home so early?"

Brandt dismissed the fact with a random wave. "I couldn't seem to stay focused on the tasks at hand. So I came home. Don't worry. I left the refinery in good hands."

The faint glow from the lamp on the other side of him

illuminated the look of reprimand on Mother's face. She slid her hands up to rest at her waist. "This wouldn't by any chance have anything to do with Miss Chambers, would it?"

He didn't have to answer that. And he wouldn't. Brandt clamped his lips tight and avoided her eyes.

"Brandt."

He squirmed. Women must receive some form of training or attend a special school to learn how to perfect that tone of voice. The one that made their sons and daughters feel like little children, no matter how old they were.

"All right." He forced out a sigh. "I admit it. I miss her. There. Are you happy?"

She gave him a soft smile. "Only because you've finally confessed your feelings. Now what are you going to do about them?"

Leaning forward in the chair and plopping his feet on the floor, he rested his elbows on his knees. Then he raked his right hand through his hair. "That's just it. I don't know."

Mother pulled the footstool a little ways away from him and sat on the edge, maintaining her proper posture. With her hands folded primly in her lap, her delicate appearance captivated him. "May I make a suggestion?"

"At this point, I'd welcome anything."

"Go to her. Talk to her. Apologize. Work it out."

Brandt gave her a half grin. "That's four suggestions."

She smiled. "You have been brooding around this house for weeks now. Ever since we returned from the island and you assumed responsibility for the refinery. This isn't good for you."

"But, Mother, we both said some rather hurtful things. And we lied to each other."

"Yes, but you both have also admitted those mistakes." She reached out and placed a hand over his. "Don't you believe it's time you laid aside your pride and sought out a way to make amends? To set things right again?"

"I don't know that I can."

"Well, son, I'm afraid that's not something I can help you do. But God can. Have you tried praying and asking for His help?"

Brandt emitted a quiet groan. That was one thing he hadn't done. No wonder his life was such a wreck.

"One thing I will say, though," Mother continued, "is you don't want to let someone like Miss Chambers get away. I almost made a mistake like that once. I don't wish you to do the same."

He snapped up his head, his eyes widening. "You, Mother? But how?"

She took a deep breath and again folded her hands in her lap. "When I first met your father, I wasn't exactly equivalent with him in social standing. It was about ten years before the War Between the States, and some of our family were involved in the local opposition against the cruel acts of the Michigan Central railroad owners." Her tongue snuck out to lick her lips before she continued. "In April of that year, the depot here in Detroit was burned to the ground. I lost an uncle almost immediately. And the way I found out was through a letter informing me that a trust fund had been established for him through my grandfather. As the oldest child of my parents—your grandparents—I was the one named to receive that inheritance."

"But how could you not know about the inheritance? He would've been the brother of one of your parents."

"The opposition to the railroad divided a lot of families, and mine was no exception. This uncle had turned his back on his family because of a disagreement over how to deal with the situation. But that didn't mean the rift couldn't be repaired. So since there were no children to inherit the fund, it went to me instead. The sudden increase in wealth now made me a viable candidate for marriage to your father. Up until that point, however, our relationship had caused a lot of problems. We almost walked away from it all."

Brandt sat back in the chair. "Wow. I had no idea."

"No, and if it weren't for this situation with Miss Chambers, you might never have been told. Your father warned you against a relationship with her because he remembered the struggle he and I faced not long ago. Just like the situation with your brother two years ago. We didn't wish for either of you to endure the same hurt. Now, though, there is no reason for not making amends. I hope this story helps you in making up your mind." With one final pat of his hand, she stood. "Don't allow the mistakes I almost made to be repeated with you. I'll be praying you make the right decision."

The door closed behind her, and Brandt sat alone. He couldn't believe what he'd just learned. His parents had almost lost their chance for the happiness they now knew. And for what? A measly measure of pride? He wouldn't let that happen to him. No matter the outcome, he was going to tell Felicity how he felt.

He only prayed she'd be receptive.

fourteen

Brandt dumped the latest refinery file from his father's accountant onto his desk. More figures and columns. Just what he didn't want at the moment. He pressed his fingers to his eyes to rid them of sleep, then slid his hands down his stubbly cheeks and chin. He'd forgotten to shave! How could he have missed that this morning?

With the few winks he'd managed to grab last night, it didn't come as too much of a surprise. During each waking period, Brandt had run several scenarios through his mind about how he'd approach Felicity. None of them sounded plausible.

There had to be an answer.

But he'd have to figure that out later. Right now he had to get over to the candle factory. His weekly meeting with Mr. Marshall was today. Maybe he could take the figures with him and have Marshall look them over. No, the man would likely peer over the rim of his glasses if Brandt made a suggestion like that. He'd get the work done. Later.

In no time at all, he reached the factory and made his way to the upper level. Marshall greeted him at the door.

"Lawson. Good to see you again. Come on in."

They made quick order of pleasantries and exchanged a brief recap of figures from the past week. It was good to hear about the success or failure of another factory. If production was low all around, he'd know it wasn't just his men.

The wooden chair protested Brandt's weight and creaked. He'd just settled back when what sounded like a small explosion and a shout came from the lower level.

"Fire!"

Brandt jumped to his feet and rushed from the office just ahead of Marshall. Rising flames drew his eyes to the far corner of the factory floor. He raced down the stairs, pausing at the bottom to follow Marshall's lead in grabbing a few coarse burlap blankets from one of the supply rooms. As he weaved through the various stations, only one thought crossed his mind.

Please, God, don't let it spread too far.

Most of the young women scattered in all directions, seeing to their own safety. A handful had already begun focusing their efforts on the fire itself by the time Brandt reached the site. Two of the supervisors cleared the area of flammable materials, and another manager attempted to keep the few remaining women at bay. Brandt tossed two blankets to the other men.

"Use them to blot out any new burning from the sparks."

Searing heat rushed in his direction, and flames licked at his clothing as he aimed straight for the center of the blaze.

"Someone get some water over here!"

An immediate flurry of activity followed his command. He prayed they'd have the intuitiveness to organize a line of volunteers, passing buckets of water from the source to the fire. In the meantime, he attacked the flames with a ferocious intensity equal to that of the small inferno.

What felt like hours likely only took about thirty minutes. They'd extinguished the last spark, and everyone breathed a sigh of relief. Black soot and scorch marks now covered everything in the immediate area. The sudden halt to the frantic pace seemed almost eerie.

Then the gradual introduction of the whirring from the machines and lye mixers penetrated Brandt's ears. One by one, the women dispersed as they realized the immediate danger no longer existed. Two or three workers remained, their heads downcast as the other three men gathered close.

Marshall regarded each one in turn. "What happened here?"

A man named Anderson stepped forward. "It appears Miss Morrow spilled a pot of boiling oils and sloshed some lye on it as well."

"But that wouldn't result in something like this." Brandt looked to Marshall for permission to get involved. The man nodded. Brandt waved his hand toward the charred remains. "Who caused the fire to start?"

A young woman spoke up next. "That would probably be my fault. I wanted to neutralize the lye spill, so I grabbed a bottle of vinegar and threw some on it."

"What's your name?"

"Brianna Fleming, sir."

"And Miss Fleming, what happened after you dispensed with the vinegar?"

She cast an eye toward one of the other girls then looked back at Brandt. "I'm afraid some of it splashed into the furnace and caused the sparks that led to the fire." She wrung her hands in front of her and shifted her weight from one foot to the other. "I truly am sorry, sir. I didn't think this would happen from such a small spill."

Brandt took a deep breath and tempered his anger. This wasn't his factory or his place to issue any reprimands. The sincerity in Miss Fleming's eyes proved her remorse. He hoped Marshall wouldn't make it worse for her. A moment later, the manager stepped forward with a reassuring smile and placed one hand on her shoulder.

"Miss Fleming, I appreciate you coming forward with your confession. I don't intend to deduct anything from your pay or Miss Morrow's." He glanced to the other girl involved then addressed everyone present. "But this only proves the necessity of adhering to the highest level of safety when attending to your workstations. We avoided a potentially more serious situation today. There is no guarantee we will be this fortunate in the future. Am I understood?"

All the workers nodded, their faces solemn.

"Now since it appears that no one was harmed, I suggest we—"

"Mr. Marshall, come quick!"

Brandt jerked his head toward the voice as Marshall asked, "Who said that?"

"Laura Price, sir. I'm down here."

Laura? And Brianna? These must be the two girls Felicity had mentioned to him.

Brandt looked at the floor where a young woman kneeled beside another figure, partially concealed from his sight by the girth of the midsized furnace. Several gasps came from the young women who craned their necks over the station as he scrambled around the equipment.

He froze as the familiar chestnut hair above a smudged face came into view. "Felicity!"

Miss Price looked up at him, her eyes wide. "You know her, too?"

He fell to his knees and quickly assessed her visible injuries. She wore a plain walking dress, but it was still of finer material than the clothes she'd worn for most of the time he'd known her. Did the girls here know who she really was? It would be best not to reveal anything about her true identity to them.

"Yes, Miss Chambers and I are"—he tried to speak past the lump in his throat—"acquainted."

Pieces of her skirt had been scorched. Soot and ash covered her one arm. Her sleeve had been torn, and reddened skin blistered from what looked like some serious burns.

"How did she come to be here? I don't believe she's worked here for weeks."

"She stopped by to visit Brianna and me, sir. We had just returned from our midmorning break when the accident happened, and she rushed to help."

Always the giver. Whether it was performing charity or lending a hand to a friend, Felicity possessed a heart of gold. How could he have been so blind? He tried to piece together a few frayed ends of her sleeve, then turned his attention to her face.

She didn't move. Didn't moan. Not a sign of life other than the slow and steady rise and fall of her chest. Tenderly he brushed back some hair from her face. A nasty bruise and small cut trickled a little blood near her ear. He withdrew his handkerchief and wiped some of the black marks from her cheeks, careful to avoid the pink areas there as well.

A gasp drew his gaze back to Miss Price. Her face registered recognition, but he didn't see how she could possibly know him. He'd only made brief visits here once a week.

"You're him! You're the refinery worker."

Her voice came out not much above a whisper. This was definitely the Laura whom Felicity had mentioned. Brandt silently pleaded with his eyes for her to remain quiet about that. She seemed to understand and nodded, but a slight grin appeared on her lips.

"I have to get Miss Chambers to the hospital."

Brandt moved into action. Placing his arms beneath Felicity's neck and legs, he scooped her into his arms and stood, shuffling for a moment or two to get his footing.

"Thanks, Lawson, for seeing to the young lady."

"My pleasure, Marshall." If only the man knew the truth. Brandt peered over the machinery. "Could you send a messenger to my father about the incident to tell him what's happened and where he can find me? I'll return if necessary to add my remarks to the incident report."

"That likely won't be necessary, but I'll get in touch with you if it is. You just take care of Miss Chambers."

The young women gaped in awe as Brandt held Felicity in his arms, searching for the quickest exit from the building. As he stepped past Laura, she gave him a quick wink.

He didn't know what Felicity had said about him, but apparently it had met with approval from this young woman.

"All right, ladies. Back to work!" Marshall's voice boomed. The rustling of clothes and the scuffling of feet answered his command.

At least the factory was once again safe and restored to order. Brandt glanced down into Felicity's pale face. If only he was as certain about Felicity.

"God, please. Let her be all right."

❧

Brandt paced back and forth in front of the private room where the nurse had taken Felicity. The doctor went into the room and came back out again three times. Not once did he provide any information or details to Brandt. When was someone going to give him another update? He just wanted to know Felicity would be all right.

"Mr. Lawson! How is she? Have you heard?"

He turned at the somewhat familiar voice of Mrs. Chambers. Mr. Chambers guided her with his arm around her waist. Worry lines furrowed her brow, and she pinned him with an earnest gaze. His own parents followed directly behind, with his brother and Felicity's sister next. Felicity's brother and another young woman brought up the rear.

The small entourage gathered around him. It pained him to tell them the truth. Perhaps with them here they could get some answers.

"I haven't heard much. It's aggravating having to stand here and watch them walk back and forth as if I'm invisible." He raked his fingers through his hair and groaned. "I haven't pressed the issue, though, as I wanted to allow the doctor as much freedom to work as possible."

"Oh, Harold. Our little girl." Mrs. Chambers buried her face against her husband's chest. He patted her back and whispered a few words to her.

"How was she when you brought her here?"

Brandt met Mr. Chambers's gaze head-on. "I have to admit, sir, she had some bad burns on her arm and a cut near her ear. Her clothes had been scorched in places." With each word he spoke, Mrs. Chambers flinched. Reporting the facts might be difficult, but it had to be done. "Other than that, she didn't seem too seriously injured. She was unconscious, though, so I couldn't tell for certain."

Mr. Chambers looked around their surroundings, appearing to take stock of the people, the hospital workers, and the possible protocol. They hadn't given Brandt a designated place to wait, so he had claimed a bench in the hall near Felicity's room as his perch. Her father turned back to him.

"And how long have you been here?"

"About an hour, sir."

Felicity's father pivoted and deposited his wife on the bench with a few quiet words to her. She nodded and took the handkerchief he offered to dab at her eyes. Mr. Chambers then stepped toward the desk where Brandt had originally spoken to a nurse about admitting Felicity.

"Let me see what I can find out," Mr. Chambers said.

His commanding presence would be enough to get anyone's attention. But the diplomatic manner in which he handled the situation struck a good balance. He reminded Brandt a lot of his own father. When these two men spoke, people listened.

Brandt prayed they'd listen enough to give them another update on Felicity.

"She's going to be all right, son." Father came to stand beside him, one hand on Brandt's shoulder. "You did the right thing, bringing her here as fast as you could. Trust the doctor to do his job."

"If only I could've done more."

Father moved to stand in front of him. "You can't live your life wondering about 'if onlys,' son. That will do nothing but pile the guilt so deep you won't be able to accomplish the tasks ahead." Father placed both hands on Brandt's shoulders. "Your mother told me about the conversation you two had yesterday."

"Yes. It helped me make up my mind about Miss Chambers."

"Son, we know you love her. It's in your eyes. Now you just have to make things right again."

Brandt *wanted* to get everything back to where they started before the visit to Mackinac Island occurred. He just didn't know if he could.

"But what if she won't see me?"

Father gave him a half smile. "I have a feeling the young lady in question will be quite amenable once she learns you rescued her."

Brandt looked across the hall at the closed door to Felicity's room. He prayed his father was right.

"All right. I was able to find out a little more about Felicity's condition," Mr. Chambers announced.

Condition? She had a condition? It must be worse than Brandt thought. She hadn't looked too bad when he brought her here. There must have been something else.

Mr. Chambers addressed everyone present, his gaze resting on each one in turn as he spoke. "They have treated her burns and the cut on her face. She was awake briefly, just long enough for them to examine her for further injuries. She had none."

A blended sigh of relief escaped from the members of both families.

Mr. Chambers continued. "A doctor should be here shortly to escort us in to see her. The nurse told me she was given a sedative to ease her pain, so she might be somewhat dazed and might not make sense."

"Since when is that such a change for Felicity?" Zach, Felicity's brother, spoke out.

A rumble of soft chuckles passed throughout the group.

"Zachary." The warning tone that accompanied his name made him flex the muscles in his neck.

Zach gave his father a sheepish grin. "Sorry."

Mr. Chambers just shook his head.

"Mr. Chambers? Mrs. Chambers?" A nurse dressed all in white, complete with a starched white head covering that reminded him of a nun's habit, addressed Felicity's parents. "My name is Nurse Kendall. If you'll come with me, I'll take you to see your daughter."

"Can we come, too?" Cecily stepped forward from the back of the group, pulling on Zach's arm and dragging him to the front as well. "She's *our* sister."

Mr. Chambers looked to the nurse, who smiled. "Of course. Please follow me."

Brandt tracked their progress down the hall and into Felicity's room. The door closed behind her family, and he once again felt like he didn't belong. Who was he to intrude on a moment that should be reserved for family alone? Her parents and brother and sister were here. They no longer needed him. Why didn't he just leave and go home?

He sank onto the bench again, dropping his head into his hands with a sigh. He ruminated on all the reasons why he should go. And he found only one reason why he should stay.

"Mr. Lawson?"

"Yes?" Brandt and his father said together.

The nurse stood before them, looking from father to son. "Oh, I'm sorry. I meant the younger Mr. Lawson."

"Yes?" Brandt repeated.

"Miss Chambers is asking for you, sir."

Felicity? Asking for him? But why?

"If you'll come with me, I'll take you to her."

Brandt cast a glance over his shoulder at his parents. Father gave him an encouraging nod, and Mother smiled softly. He turned back to where Nurse Kendall stood waiting. There didn't seem to be any other option. He had no choice. Isn't this what he'd wanted? Isn't this why he'd stayed and waited? So then why did his feet all of a sudden feel like two large bricks?

"Mr. Lawson? If you please."

Nurse Kendall extended her hand, palm up, toward Brandt. Through no will of his own, he followed. As they reached the door, it opened and out came Felicity's family. Brandt licked his lips several times and swallowed. They all gave him a look he couldn't decipher before moving past him and continuing down the hall.

Brandt took a step forward and stopped when Mr. Chambers placed a hand on his shoulder. The man didn't say a word. He only spread his lips into a slight grin then went to join his family.

The time had come. The moment of reckoning hovered over his head like a cloud.

God, please give me strength and the right words to say.

Nurse Kendall pushed the door open a crack and stepped back to allow him entrance. Brandt placed one foot in front of the other and jumped when the door clicked closed behind him. Rays of light filtered through the sheer curtains at the windows. His eyes immediately sought the single bed and the young woman lying in it.

Her eyes were closed, and she didn't open them at his entrance. Even though she had bandages on her arms and face, he had never seen Felicity look so beautiful. With caution, Brandt approached the bedside where she lay. She mumbled and smacked her lips together. Her left hand raised and settled across her abdomen. A wince accompanied the movement.

Brandt rushed to her side and reached for the pitcher of water on the table. He poured a glass and held it to her lips, slipping his free arm behind her head and lifting her to drink. Any moment now, she would see him there. What would he do then? Her eyelids fluttered as she took a few sips then relaxed against his arm. He laid her back against the pillows and returned the glass to the table.

"Mmm." She smacked her lips again. "Thank you."

"You're welcome." His voice cracked, and the two words came out in a combination cough and squeak. Brandt took a seat in the empty chair next to him, cleared his throat, and tried again. "You're welcome."

Felicity opened her eyes and turned her head to look at him. A soft smile formed on her lips. "Brandt." She slid her hand off her stomach and to the bedside. The muscles in her neck strained as she tried to move her arm more.

Brandt covered her hand with his and placed his other on her forearm, just below the bandages. "No, no. Don't try to move. Just rest."

"I'm so glad you came." Her voice was so soft he had to lean closer to hear her. "Thank you." She swallowed. "Thank you for rescuing me."

"I'm just glad I was there at all." Despite what his father said, Brandt couldn't keep the self-condemnation from his voice.

Felicity closed her eyes for a moment. The soft sounds of

her breathing accompanied the faint noises from the hallway. When her eyelids opened again, the same doubt, uncertainty, and fear he felt reflected back at him from her deep pools.

"Brandt, I have something—"

"Shh." He cut her off and touched two fingers to her lips, then removed his hand. She stared at him with doelike innocence. "Let me go first."

An almost imperceptible nod followed his entreaty. All right. He had her undivided attention. Now what should he say?

"Felicity, I have been repeating in my mind the last conversation we had. And I owe you an apology." There, that wasn't such a bad start. "We both made it clear that night that we had our reasons for doing what we did. I am just as guilty as I accused you of being. I was wrong for lying and wrong for getting so angry with you. You deserve more than that." He implored her with his gaze and gave her hand a tender squeeze. "Can you ever forgive me?"

It hadn't come out the way he'd rehearsed it in his head, but it could still work. At least he hoped it would.

Felicity's hand moved beneath his, and she turned her wrist to interlace their fingers. He glanced down at their joined hands then back at her face. Tenderness replaced the uncertainty of a moment before.

"Yes," she whispered. "I forgive you." A small fit of coughs started in her chest, and her body shook.

Brandt poured another glass of water for her. When she finished, she again settled back against the pillows, reaching for his hand once more.

"I was also wrong for being dishonest and in blaming you. Can *you* forgive *me*?"

He didn't hesitate. "Yes. Of course I will." How could he deny her what she'd just given him?

She visibly relaxed. Her entire body sank farther into the mattress, and her expression seemed much more at peace. As she started to close her eyes, Brandt tightened his hold on her wrist. He had to get this out now, or he might lose his nerve. Felicity rolled her head to the left and looked at him.

"There. . .there's one more thing."

Her eyes seemed to tell him to go on, but the words died in his throat. Maybe making her smile would lighten the mood a bit and help him say what he'd come to tell her.

"At least I know I have a captive audience this time."

That worked. Her slow grin turned into a full smile that reached all the way to her eyes. Yes. That's just what he needed to help him get through the next part of his confession. After unlacing their fingers, Brandt clasped her hand between both of his.

"Felicity, it took our parents' schemes to make me realize just how special you are to me. I'm a fool for not seeing it sooner." He sought her gaze and held it. "Maybe I didn't want to believe it. Maybe I wasn't ready. I don't know. What I do know is I don't want to lose you."

A sharp gasp followed his declaration. This was it. He had to say it now.

"Felicity, I love you. I've probably loved you for a while now. I was just too blind to see it."

Her lips moved, but no sound came out. Then she seemed to find her voice.

"Brandt. I love you, too."

This was going better than he thought. He grinned and slid to one knee on the floor. "Then will you marry me?"

"Yes!"

Brandt rose and leaned over her to give her a quick peck on the mouth. He pulled back to look down into her face, seeing the same longing he felt inside. Lowering his lips again, he positioned himself for a better kiss this time.

"Splendid!"

"Excellent!"

"It's about time!"

Exclamations of delight and enthusiasm accompanied the clapping of hands. Brandt whipped around, almost losing his balance. There, crowding the doorway, stood both his and Felicity's families. With wide grins and beaming smiles and the small applause, they gave their obvious approval of this new relationship. Far more than the friends they were, Brandt and Felicity now moved on to a newfound love.

He chuckled and turned his chair parallel to the bed before sitting down. Grabbing her hand once more, he shared a special look with her, emboldened by her nod and the look of love in her eyes.

"You all obviously heard. And we know what you think. Now will you perhaps leave us alone to discuss a few more things?"

Cecily pushed everyone else aside and strode into the room. "There will be time enough for that later. Right now we want to celebrate with you both."

The two families voiced their agreement, and all followed Cecily's lead. Oh well. At least they had their privacy for a few moments.

Brandt pivoted to face Felicity. Amusement danced in her eyes. He shrugged. They could discuss the details of the wedding and their engagement another time. Right now they had their families together, and their relationship had been restored. God had smiled down upon them, despite their bumbled attempts to handle things themselves. Anything else would just have to wait.

epilogue

Felicity leaned back against Brandt, his arms enfolding her against his chest. "Mmm, I can't believe it's been almost a year already." Normally Molly would accompany her as a chaperone, but Mother had granted permission for them to have this evening to themselves. The rare moment of freedom after a year of being watched was a welcome pleasure.

"A year since what?" Brandt's warm breath fanned across her hair and stirred a few loose strands.

She giggled. "Since you asked me to become your wife, silly."

She felt his smile against her head. "Oh, that."

"Oh, that?" Felicity sat up and pivoted to stare at him. "You make it sound like it's nothing of consequence. Like it's a normal, everyday occurrence." She placed her hands on her hips. "Tell me, Mr. Lawson, just how many women have you proposed to in your life?"

The rumbling chuckle started in his chest and burst forth as a full-fledged laugh by the time it reached his mouth. Amusement danced in his eyes as he reached for her hands, raising first one then the other to his lips. The intensity in his eyes made her quiver inside.

"Only one, my dear. And that's the only one I intend to ask." The corner of his mouth turned up as he smirked. "Besides, with your tendency to masquerade as someone other than your true self, you are more than enough for me to handle."

She grinned. "I haven't engaged in any behavior such as that since last summer. And you know it."

Brandt drew lazy circles on the backs of her hands with his thumbs. They'd come to the lakeshore and chosen this spot by the tree to ensure some final moments of privacy before the wedding tomorrow. At times the year had seemed to drag, but with all the details to plan for the elaborate affair Mother had insisted on having, the time passed more quickly than Felicity had expected. She and Brandt both had suggested something smaller, but Mother would have none of that. Even now a few final details flitted through Felicity's mind, but Brandt didn't seem interested in talking about them. If he intended to distract her, he was doing an excellent job.

All of a sudden he dropped her hands and sat up straight, twisting to reach for the satchel he'd brought with them.

"I was wondering when we'd get around to finding out what you have in there." Felicity raised her chin and leaned toward him, attempting to see inside.

Brandt held up one finger. "Nuh-uh. No peeking. It's a surprise."

Returning to her previous position, she tucked her legs close to her side. Felicity clasped her hands together and forced them into her lap. Anticipation made her want to squeal for Brandt to hurry, but she managed a docile tone instead.

"I do so love surprises."

Brandt reached into the satchel and withdrew a thin cardboard box. "And this is one I know you're going to treasure." He handed it to her.

Felicity almost dropped it. "Goodness, it's heavy!" She hadn't expected such weight from something that appeared so simple.

"I assure you it will be worth its weight in gold."

She tipped her head and regarded him for a moment. He seemed so sure of himself, so confident she would love this. What had he gone and done now?

"Well, are you going to open it or not?"

He sounded as eager as she felt. "All right." She smiled, allowing her excitement to once again bubble within. "I'll open it now."

Taking great care, she slid her thumb along the edge of the lid and underneath the flap. With that flipped up, Felicity then reached inside to pull out the object, wrapped in white tissue paper and nestled amid a bit of straw. Another quick glance at Brandt showed a light in his eyes as he watched her unveil his gift.

She pulled back the top part of the tissue paper and gasped. "Brandt! How did you know?"

The jeweled egg! Rushing to pull away the remainder of the tissue, Felicity bit her lip and bounced in place. Moisture gathered at the corners of her eyes, and she raised her blurry gaze to his.

He reached out and caressed her cheek. "A little birdie told me you might want to add this piece to your collection."

"Cecily."

Brandt nodded. "One and the same." He implored her with an earnest gaze. "So do you like it?"

Felicity leaned forward and threw her arms around him. "Oh, Brandt, I absolutely love it!"

He unwound her arms from his neck and settled her back in place. "Well then, there's one more thing I must show you."

"There's more?"

Brandt placed both hands on the egg and opened the clasp. Soft music started to play as the little box turned. He put his thumb on the golden bow at the front and pulled back, revealing another little compartment tucked away within the box. Feeling like a little girl, Felicity tilted the egg toward her. A cry accompanied her sharp intake of breath.

There, set in a tiny piece of velvet, sat a lone golden band. Felicity had no words to say. Emotion choked them off.

"I was going to present this gift earlier, but considering where you first saw this and where we're to be married tomorrow, I altered my plans. I hope you don't mind."

Felicity picked up the ring and held it in her hand for further inspection. The polished gold gleamed in the sunlight. Tears again gathered in her eyes, and one or two spilled down her cheeks. She sniffed and slid her gaze from the ring to Brandt's face.

"Oh, Brandt." She pushed up on her knees and hugged him, whispering against his ear, "You've made me so happy!"

Brandt pulled her close in a tight embrace. They sat there for several moments, Felicity basking in his warmth and the security and comfort of his love.

He cleared his throat. "All right. I think we'd better go for a walk along the lakeshore. Otherwise I might forget that we marry *tomorrow* and do something improper."

Felicity giggled and pulled away. After allowing him to help her stand, she tucked her right hand into the crook of his elbow. He gathered the egg and box and led them out of the gazebo. She held her left hand out in front of her, admiring the beauty and simplicity of her engagement ring again. The gold band would only add to the symbol of Brandt's love. Tomorrow they would speak their vows and become husband and wife. But for now and today, she couldn't be happier.

❧

"As copper must endure a refining process to bring out its luster, as a candle must be shaped and molded before its true beauty shines forth, so your two lives will undergo the same transformation as you grow in love and understanding of each other."

The preacher stood in front of Brandt and Felicity, admonishing them to love, honor, and cherish each other and to place their union second only to their service and devotion to God. They could have been married by the parson on the island, but Brandt wanted Felicity's pastor to do the honors. He'd been attending her church since he proposed. Preacher Westcott had offered some sound spiritual wisdom once or twice, and Brandt could think of no one better.

Felicity's hands fit snugly into his as he faced the woman who would soon become his wife. He couldn't take his eyes off her. Through her veil, he could see a clouded image of her face. Her hair had been styled and gathered on top of her head, with a single wide curl resting over her left shoulder. The sparkle in her eyes no doubt mirrored the light in his.

They'd finally made it.

After they had repeated their vows to each other, the preacher looked at them both and said, "You may now add your personal promises."

At Westcott's invitation, Brandt raised Felicity's hands a few inches and took a step forward.

"We began our journey together as friends, and although we had some rocky roads in the middle, our love saw us through. I chose this spot for us since it's the place where our lives unraveled and everything fell apart." He swallowed past the tightness in his throat and forced his voice to remain strong. "Today we stand here before God, family, and friends to put it all back together. I pledge my undying love to you and will give my life to see you happy."

Felicity inhaled a shuddering breath to speak her answering vows. "From the start, you became a friend, a confidant, and a person in whom I could see true integrity. We survived the fire of our mistakes and arose from the ashes stronger for the experience." She sniffed. "This day I pledge my lifelong love and devotion, promising to honor and respect you above all others, and believing in God to guide us from here forward."

They exchanged rings after the preacher blessed them, and

Brandt covered Felicity's hands with his own.

"Having pledged themselves to each other through their individual vows and through the giving and receiving of their rings, Mr. Brandt Lawson and Miss Felicity Chambers are now joined. By the powers vested in me by the State of Michigan and bestowed by our almighty Father, I now pronounce you husband and wife. What therefore God hath joined together, let not man put asunder." Preacher Westcott beamed a wide grin. "You may now kiss your bride."

Those were the best six words he'd heard all day. Brandt fingered the fine lace of Felicity's veil and raised it to reveal her beautiful face. Unabashed tears filled her eyes, but a smile from ear to ear showed her joy. Framing her face with both of his hands, he leaned forward and touched his lips to hers once, then twice, then a final time that sealed the promise of the vows they'd spoken.

Cheers and applause rose from the expansive crowd of family and friends gathered to witness the ceremony. Brandt pulled back—albeit with reluctance—and turned them both to gaze out at the sea of faces. Felicity slipped her hand into his, and he gave it a squeeze. The day couldn't be more perfect. They had God's favor once again and their families' continued support.

From this day forward, they'd weather any storm—together.

A Letter To Our Readers

Dear Reader:
In order that we might better contribute to your reading enjoyment, we would appreciate your taking a few minutes to respond to the following questions. We welcome your comments and read each form and letter we receive. When completed, please return to the following:

Fiction Editor
Heartsong Presents
PO Box 719
Uhrichsville, Ohio 44683

1. Did you enjoy reading *Copper and Candles* by Amber Stockton?
   ❏ Very much! I would like to see more books by this author!
   ❏ Moderately. I would have enjoyed it more if

   _____

   _____

   _____

2. Are you a member of **Heartsong Presents**? ❏ Yes ❏ No
   If no, where did you purchase this book? _____

   _____

3. How would you rate, on a scale from 1 (poor) to 5 (superior), the cover design? _____

4. On a scale from 1 (poor) to 10 (superior), please rate the following elements.

   ____ Heroine   ____ Plot
   ____ Hero   ____ Inspirational theme
   ____ Setting   ____ Secondary characters

5. These characters were special because? _____

_____

_____

6. How has this book inspired your life? _____

_____

_____

7. What settings would you like to see covered in future
Heartsong Presents books? _____

_____

_____

8. What are some inspirational themes you would like to see
treated in future books? _____

_____

_____

9. Would you be interested in reading other **Heartsong
Presents** titles? ❑ Yes ❑ No

10. Please check your age range:
    ❑ Under 18   ❑ 18-24
    ❑ 25-34   ❑ 35-45
    ❑ 46-55   ❑ Over 55

Name_____

Occupation _____

Address _____

City, State, Zip_____

All aboard! Next stop—
Texas, where love derails
the best-laid plans of
a reluctant rancher, a
meddlesome schoolmarm,
and two children on an
orphan train.

Historical, paperback, 288 pages, 5⁵⁄₁₆" x 8"